GETTING OUT

A POST-APOCALYPTIC EMP SURVIVAL THRILLER - THE EMP BOOK 1

RYAN WESTFIELD

1

MAX

Max sat in his cubicle with his chair pointed to the window. He'd been staring outside for the last twenty minutes, unable to concentrate on his work. On the best days, the work seemed pointless. On the worst, it was a nightmare.

It was supposed to be a good job, decent pay, good benefits. He had a real "career," unlike some of his friends, who were still working odd jobs here and there. If his parents had been alive, they would have been proud of him.

But it wasn't what he wanted to do. The problem? He didn't know *what* he wanted to do. He only knew that things didn't feel right. Something was wrong with the world, and Max already knew that it wasn't going to get any better.

"Psst, Max," whispered Jeremy, his cubicle neighbor.

"Huh?" said Max, waking up from his little daydream.

"You've been staring out the window for like forever, man," said Jeremy. "Big Tom is going to come around soon, you know."

"Screw Big Tom," said Max. Big Tom was the boss, a guy with a much bigger gut than a heart. Max figured him for some kind of sadist who'd happened to get into the line of work that allowed him to pursue his true passion—torturing his employees with meaningless reports and "metrics," whatever the hell those were.

"What's that?" said Big Tom, moving slowly into view, blocking Max's view of the window.

"Shit," muttered Jeremy nervously. He immediately hunched back over his desk and started working furiously on some meaningless project.

"Hi, Tom," said Max calmly. He wasn't in the mood today to really give a shit about any of this. Maybe he should just quit, and head up to the old farmhouse that his dad had left him when he'd passed away. Max had been meaning to head up there and check the place out for a while. The old house hadn't been used in years, but Max had been toying with the fantasy of creating a homestead there. The only problem? He didn't know much about homesteading, having grown up in the suburbs away from real nature.

"I heard what you said," hissed Big Tom, leaning down towards Max, bracing his hands on his khaki-covered knees.

"Yeah?" said Max.

Suddenly, something happened.

The lights went out. Everything went out.

A tremendous silence hung in the air.

"What was that?" said Big Tom, standing up straight and looking around.

Max swiveled his chair around to face his computer again. He felt as if he was expecting something... He had a feeling about what happened, but his mind couldn't put it directly into thoughts.

The computer was completely blank. Dead.

Max hit the power button, but nothing happened.

"Someone cut the electricity," shouted Big Tom.

Max looked around, seeing that everyone else's computers were dead as well. Max picked up the phone. There wasn't a dial tone. Hastily, he took his phone out of his pocket, but the screen was black.

"It's not just the power," Max said.

"They're going to pay for this," shouted Big Tom again. "Don't they realize how much money we'll lose?"

Max sat still in his chair for a moment.

So it was happening.

This was what he'd been thinking about for two years now: some kind of EMP event. Max didn't exactly understand the specifics, but he knew that, given the right circumstances, solar flares on the sun could create electromagnetic pulses strong enough to wipe out most electronics on Earth.

This was a big part of the malaise he'd been feeling for so long: he knew that something was very wrong in the world. The infrastructure was simply too fragile. Everything relied on a shipping system, and everything relied on electronics that could easily be disabled or promptly deactivated with an EMP. Or something else. There were a million things that could happen that could cause a cataclysmic shutdown of modern society, and Max had spent hours on the internet reading about them all.

That didn't mean he was *exactly* prepared for an event.

But perhaps he was a little more prepared than most. At home, he had a rudimentary bug out bag that he'd started preparing. In it, he had a basic medical kit, some veterinary antibiotics, a hunting knife, an axe, and a couple odds and ends he'd assembled over the years. It wasn't a complete kit, and when Max's thoughts turned to it in this moment, he cursed himself for not having gone whole hog on the idea.

Max knew it was time to act.

Everyone in the office was starting to panic, as they

pulled out their cell phones and realized that they all didn't work. They realized, unlike the boss, Big Tom, that this wasn't just a mere power outage. Soon, everyone in Claymore would be panicking, all trying to drive home. The roads would be blocked off.

Max had one thing on his mind: get home, get his gear, and high tail it to the old farmhouse, where he'd be away from the panic and chaos that would ensue.

Max was surprised how calm he felt, and how quickly his mind went right to the solution. He knew this was his advantage, and that everyone else would take days, if not weeks, to come to the same conclusion.

Max got up from his swivel chair so quickly that it slammed right into his desk, making a huge noise.

Since no machines or electronics were running, the room had fallen deafeningly silent, except for the mutterings of the boss. Everyone else sat frightened in their cubicles, unmoving, perhaps whispering to each other.

Max's chair made a surprisingly loud sound against the background of dead silence.

"Where do you think you're going, Max?" shouted Big Tom.

"Home," said Max, deadpan.

"Dude," whispered Jeremy, looking up at Max from his chair. "Sit back down if you want a job. He's in a bad mood."

"So am I," said Max.

Max ignored his colleagues and darted towards the exit. It was deadly silent. No one was even whispering.

The overhead lights were of course off, natural light streaming in from the office windows.

Big Tom moved swiftly to block his way. He stood in front of Max in the doorway to the exit.

Max could feel that all eyes were on him.

One of the precautions he'd taken a year ago, when he'd started getting more into a mindset of preparedness, was to carry a few important and practical possessions with him at all times. One was his well-oiled pocket knife with a thumb stud. The other was his Glock 17, which sat hidden in his holster inside the waist band of his pants, with his shirt untucked and covering it. It was considered by some too big to carry daily, but Max had found that once he'd gotten used to it, he didn't mind it. Most of the time, he knew it was there, but he liked the feeling of the weight and heft against his hip.

But Max had a calm head, and he wasn't about to shoot his boss for merely getting in his way. He knew that Big Tom wasn't a serious danger. He was just a nuisance. The real dangers would come in the coming days, provided the power wasn't restored, and considering the nature of an EMP, Max knew that that wasn't possible.

"Get out of my way," said Max in a low and calm voice, but one that meant business.

"You walk out that door, Max, and you're out a job," hissed Big Tom. He tried to stand up tall, puffing up his chest. But Max wasn't the least bit intimidated.

"Don't you get it?" said Max. "This isn't just a power outage. Don't you see that everything's off? Check your cell phone. This is the end of the world we've been living in."

"You're crazy," said Big Tom. But he sounded scared. "I'm telling you, Max. Walk out that door now, and that's the last straw. You've spent too many days staring out the window. One more demerit on your record and you're done. And forget about a recommendation."

Max just shook his head in disbelief. He knew people would be slow to catch on, but actually confronting the reality of it was... astounding.

"Out of my way now," said Max.

Big Tom bowed his head slightly, looking at the ground before stepping aside.

Max was in good physical condition, and Tom could sense that he wasn't a match for Max, not that he'd ever dream of fighting him. Fighting wasn't part of the modern cultured world, especially not in an office environment. Instead of thinking about physical capabilities, Big Tom's managerial head was likely instead filled with ideas about potential lawsuits and demerits of his own that he'd have to deal with, should he find himself in a physical altercation.

Max walked out of the office. He knew it would be the last time.

The door slammed behind him, louder than anything he'd heard in the intense silence surrounding him.

The lights were off in the staircase.

He took a single cautious step past the threshold and paused. When he closed his eyes, he couldn't tell the difference. That was how dark it was.

There, in the silent darkness of the stairwell, the reality suddenly struck him. His heart started pounding in his chest. The anxiety hit him like a tidal wave. His pulse skyrocketed and his skin felt cold and clammy.

He'd had it together back in the office. He'd been vaguely planning this for years, or at least considering the possibility. He had some gear at home, and he had a plan, unlike a lot of other people. He had enough food for over a month.

But suddenly, none of it felt like it would be enough.

And he was all alone, the silent, dark staircase reinforcing this thought.

Was he really better off than anyone else, or would he become trapped like the rest of them, left to die a slow death of hunger, or perhaps something worse? After all, he still had no idea what had happened.

Max tried to reach into his pocket for his LED flashlight, hoping against hope that it hadn't been affected by the EMP. But his hand was trembling too much, and he couldn't even slide it into the pocket of his jeans.

Shit. That was all he could think: shit. His mind was stuck in a loop of panic.

2

MANDY

andy had taken the day off from work. She'd
managed to wake up early enough to call in,
doing her best impression of a sore throat. "I
can come in if you really need me," she'd said. "But I think I
might be contagious. You don't want to see what I just did to
the toilet."

"All right, all right, spare us the details," her boss had
said, laughing. "Come in tomorrow if you're feeling better.
Make sure you call me at the end of the day to let me know
how you're doing. I'll have to get Rachel to cover your
shift, shit..."

Mandy had let out a big sigh of relief and let her head
fall back on her pillow. She'd fallen back into half-drunk
dreams, where nothing seemed to happen and everything
felt static and strange.

At noon, she woke up again, her head pounding from
the beers she'd had the night before at the bar. She knocked
over the lamp from her nightstand getting out of bed, and
stepped right onto a glass of water that she must have left on
the floor the night before.

Stumbling into the bathroom, she flicked the light switch, but nothing happened. That was weird. Maybe the bulb was out. She pulled open the blinds to let in enough light to find the aspirin bottle in the medicine cabinet.

She shook out a handful, not bothering to count them, and swallowed them with a glass of water that had been sitting out for probably a week.

She stumbled into the kitchen, where she flipped the light switch. No lights again. She cursed under her breath. The power must be out again in the apartment building. It hadn't happened in a while.

The last time it had gone out, she'd been living with Ted, her boyfriend of five years, who she'd just broken up with.

She shuddered at the memory of her and Ted huddling under a blanket, playing cards with a flashlight propped up like a lantern.

The memories were still fresh and painful. That was why she'd been out drinking last night with some friends from her old job, who'd promised to take her out and make her forget all about her problems. It hadn't quite worked out like that, and the main thing Mandy remembered from the end of the night was crying in someone's arms, drunkenly sobbing about Ted. Ted was long gone, out somewhere in California with his new girlfriend.

Despite her headache, the power outage, and her breakup, not to mention the shitty job she was barely holding onto, Mandy was a woman of internal resources. She decided right then and there to get things going today. She surveyed the apartment, which was a disaster. Normally clean and pristine, it was now full of ice cream containers that she hadn't even bothered to throw out. The dirty dishes piled up out of the sink and onto the counter.

She poured coffee into the automatic coffee maker and hit the button before remembering that the power was out.

There was a knock at the door, loud and forceful.

"Who is it?" she said sleepily, winding through the mess on the floor of her apartment towards the door.

"Who is it?" she said again, peering through the peephole.

"Mrs. Kerns," came the reply.

Mrs. Kerns was an older retired woman who lived on the same floor as Mandy. It was just the three of them on the second floor: Mandy, Mrs. Kerns, and a single man named Max, who Mandy hadn't ever exchanged more than a few words with. He always seemed so serious, and perhaps a little too disgruntled to have a friendly conversation with.

Mandy groaned internally. She didn't want to deal with Mrs. Kerns right now. Sure, she was a nice old lady, in most respects, but she was *not* the type of person that Mandy wanted to deal with when she was hung over. And surely Mrs. Kerns would want Mandy to contact the landlord or something.

Mandy paused before opening the door, trying to fix something of a smile on her face. Then she remembered she shouldn't be waking up at noon, and she sure as hell looked like she'd just woken up. She remembered vaguely calling work and pretending to be sick, so she tried to fix her face into whatever a "sick" expression was before opening the door.

"Mrs. Kerns," she said, trying to make her voice sound a little scratchy, opening the door wide.

"What's happened to you, dear?" said Mrs. Kerns. "Did you lose power too? Why aren't you at work?"

Mandy felt immediately overwhelmed with the peppering questions, and wished she'd just pretended she hadn't been at home. Why didn't she think of that? It wasn't like Mrs. Kerns would have seen that the lights were on.

"I don't have power either," said Mandy, after a long pause. "I'm sick."

She hoped that would cover her disarray.

"Might I come in, dear?" said Mrs. Kerns, in that pushy way that older ladies could sometimes so naturally be.

"Um," said Mandy. "It's a little messy."

"My back is killing me, and I left the cane in my apartment."

Sighing, Mandy stepped aside to let Mrs. Kerns into the apartment.

"My God!" exclaimed Mrs. Kerns upon seeing the horrible mess.

"Yeah," said Mandy. "Sorry about the mess... It's been a tough week."

"Oh, yes, I almost forgot... I heard about Ted."

Did the whole building know her personal business? Did everyone know that she'd caught Ted cheating on her, talking to his online girlfriend over the internet? Did they all know that Mandy wasn't exactly sure who'd broken up with who, whether Ted had left her or whether she'd thrown him out of the house?

The two of them sat down on the couch. Mandy hurried to move aside her half-opened laptop and some old magazines that she'd partially torn up in a bad mixture of anger and depression.

"I was going to call the landlord soon," said Mandy, anticipating Mrs. Kerns's next question.

"I already did," said Mrs. Kerns, in a matter of fact way. "Well, I tried to, but the phones are all dead."

"Do you have a cell phone?"

"I'm not *that* old, am I?" said Mrs. Kerns. "Of course I do."

"Let me try my phone. I'll be back in a second."

She went into her bedroom to get her phone. She picked it up, and noticed that the screen was dead.

She went back into the living room.

"That's strange," she said, sitting back down on the couch. "I remember distinctly that I charged it last night at the, um, bar."

"Everything's dead," said Mrs. Kerns.

"What do you mean everything's dead?"

"All the machines. All the electronics. None of them work. I've been downstairs to see Alison, and none of her things work either. And I even looked out to the other buildings. There isn't a single light on. But the strangest thing is that if you look out to the other buildings—I can see over to Downing Street from my living room window—none of the lights are on either. And the Nevins are always home, with all the lights always on."

"Hmm," said Mandy. "I guess the whole town lost power. I mean, that's happened before, but usually it's when there's a storm..."

Mrs. Kerns shook her head. "There wasn't a storm."

"Maybe a transformer or something?" said Mandy. She only vaguely knew what a transformer was, but she knew it had something to do with electricity.

Mrs. Kerns shook her head. "I don't know. But I'm worried. I've never seen anything like this."

Mandy didn't know what to think, but she was starting to get nervous. "This is really weird," she said. "Oh, what about the radio?"

Mrs. Kerns shook her head again. "I tried," she said. "It doesn't work. Just like all the machines. I guess my father was right. He was always telling us that these gadgets wouldn't save us."

"There's something!" said Mandy. "I heard something outside. Sounds like cars."

They both stopped speaking.

Mandy moved to the window and pushed the slats of the blinds aside to peer outside to the parking lot. Most of the cars were gone. Most of the residents were at work, after all. Her own car sat there, a beat up old Honda Civic with dents all over it. It must have been at least fifteen years old, but that was what Mandy could afford with her waitressing job.

They could clearly hear the sound of car engines approaching. But Mandy didn't see anything yet. There was something odd about the sound. They sounded bigger, beefier than normal engines.

"Someone's coming," whispered Mandy.

"Shh," said Mrs. Kerns.

A single truck pulled slowly into the parking lot. It didn't look like any truck that Mandy would have seen in her normal life. It was a military style truck, something like a beefy pickup. It was painted a solid light green color, without any camouflage. There were two or three men up in the front cab, and a man in the back manning a huge turret gun.

Mandy gasped. She'd never seen anything like this in the United States. It reminded her of the trip she'd taken in high school to Mexico for spring break. There, she'd been shocked to see the police driving around town in pickup trucks with guns mounted on the back. Honestly, though, she'd been too drunk to remember much else from the trip. Not that she was a big drinker. She'd barely had a drink since she'd dropped out of college after her first disastrous semester, except for yesterday night.

Mandy watched for a moment as the truck slowly circled the parking lot. The man in the back of the truck seemed to be scanning the area. For what, Mandy didn't know.

There weren't any markings on the truck that she could see.

The men looked like they might be from the United States Army, but she couldn't get a good look at them.

She had a bad feeling in her stomach, and it wasn't the beer she drank last night. She kept moving her face away from the window, worried that they would see her.

"What's going on?" said Mrs. Kerns, starting to get up slowly from the couch.

"Shh," whispered Mandy, waving her hand for Mrs. Kerns to stay where she was.

Mandy didn't know who these men were or what they were doing here, but she had a feeling that it wouldn't be good if they knew she was here... at least not until she knew what they were up to.

3

MAX

Max had finally gotten over his mild panic attack, or whatever you wanted to call it. He cursed himself under his breath for being weak. This wasn't the time to freak out. This was the time for action, for making logical choices.

The rest of his coworkers were still up in the office. Max didn't see a single person in the parking lot as he walked to his Jeep 4x4, an old but reliable car. He'd done all the recent repairs on it himself, and he knew he could rely on it in times like this.

The only thing was... would it start after an EMP?

Max was pretty sure it would. He'd spent too many hours online, reading about these sorts of things, and the general consensus seemed to be that the majority of cars would start after an EMP. Some newer cars might have electronics problems, but Max's Jeep didn't have any of that new fancy nonsense.

Still, despite how much he trusted the car, he breathed a sigh of relief as the engine roared to life when he turned the key in the ignition.

"There we go," muttered Max, to the car as much as himself, as he pulled out of the parking lot.

Max was glad he hadn't taken that job in the city. He shuddered to think what must be going on in Philly. Or what might happen in the coming days. If this was what Max was pretty sure it was, no food would be arriving. And in the city, plenty of people had guns... It would quickly descend into complete chaos as people who'd never experienced true hunger suddenly were cut off from their cheeseburgers and potato chips.

Out on the road, everything looked surprisingly normal.

Just the calm before the storm, thought Max.

There were one or two cars out along with Max. Pretty typical for this time of day, although normally there might be more.

The traffic lights were all out, but Max didn't see any police doing normal traffic work. No, they'd be busier with other things.

Max flicked the radio on, expecting nothing but static. Instead, the radio didn't even turn on. It was fried.

It was strange to feel so *cut off*. Max was something of a lone wolf in general, but in this moment, he felt more isolated than he ever had before. Seeing the dead faces of the office buildings and the stores was strange and eerie. And no one was out. That was the strangest thing. Normally there'd be people walking their dogs, going on jogs. Max didn't see a single person walking around.

He drove slowly towards his apartment. He knew he didn't have much time before things really started happening, but he also wanted to drive cautiously. The last thing he needed right now was some problem with the Jeep.

He knew it was only too easy to do something careless, like running over something unexpected in the road, especially when dealing with a stressful situation like this. The last thing he needed was for the Jeep to be out of commission. He had to get to the farmhouse in Lampton, PA, about eight hours away on a normal day. And this was not a normal day. Who know how long it would take for Max to make it there.

Max looked behind him in the rearview mirror. He could hear the sound of a big truck coming up behind him.

It passed him going about sixty miles an hour on what was normally a low-speed road. It was a military cargo truck, probably full of soldiers.

Max just kept driving normally, although he made sure to stay as far over to the shoulder as possible.

He was only a couple minutes from his apartment building, when he came to a police barricade.

There was a single cop standing in the road. Not near a traffic light or anything, just in the middle of the road. His police cruiser was parked sideways on the road, and he had the rest of the road blocked off with yellow crime scene tape and a couple folding chairs. Pretty shabby for the local police, who were known for having a higher than normal budget, especially considering the low crime in the area.

Max wasn't worried. It wasn't like the cop was going to arrest him.

That said, Max didn't know how the military and police were going to handle this new crisis. Maybe they'd enforce road blocks, or some kind of curfew. Something like that could interfere with Max's plans to leave the area.

But there was no doubt in Max's mind that he would do whatever it took to get out. Staying there would be certain slow death. Without the shipping system, no food would arrive, and chaos would ensue. The police and military would only be able to contain the masses for so long.

Max pulled up slowly to the police officer, who Max noted had his hand already on the handle of his pistol.

"What's going on, officer?" said Max, in his most polite tone. He tried to act just like a normal concerned civilian, who would do whatever he was told by an authority figure.

The cop didn't answer him. He just gave him a steely stare.

"License or identification," said the cop.

This was a big departure from the standard "license and registration." It meant they already weren't concerned with who was driving what.

Max realized suddenly that the cop's radio wouldn't work. He doubted the cops would have taken the precautions of shielding some two way radios from possible EMP blasts.

Max took out his wallet and handed the cop his ID.

"What's your destination?" said the cop, not breaking from his deadpan voice and stare.

"Just heading back to my apartment," said Max. "I work on a computer all day. So, you know, there wasn't any power so I figured I'd just take the day off." He gave a little laugh at the end to try to show that he was just a regular guy who wasn't up to anything. He figured the authorities would want everyone to stay home.

The cop nodded at him and handed the license back.

"Any weapons?" he said.

Max laughed. "Nope," he said. "Never was the type. My girlfriend was all anti-NRA and everything. She would never let me have one." Of course, he didn't have a girlfriend.

The cop looked at him, studying him.

Max wondered if he was going to get a pat down. If he did, it'd be beyond easy to find the Glock in his waistband.

Max tried his best to look relaxed, innocent, and clueless.

He'd only ever used the Glock at the firing range. But today was the day, of all days, when he really needed it. Max knew that there might come a time soon when the Glock would be what stood between life and death.

What measures would he be willing to take to keep the gun?

The cop kept staring at him.

Finally, after what seemed like an eternity, he turned his gaze to the car behind Max, giving Max a brisk wave of his hand to signal that he should continue onward.

"Thanks, officer," called out Max, cheerily.

But Max's fake smile turned to an expression of grim determination.

He could already see that it had started: the police were going to have their own agenda, and it wasn't going to be in Max's best interest to adhere to whatever rules they put in place. They would soon become fractured without radios, without a central guiding principle. Max wondered what principles they were operating under right now.

He pulled into the large parking lot of his apartment building, just as a military truck was pulling out. It drove slowly. There was a turret gun, manned by a soldier, in the bed of the extra large pickup. It wasn't any civilian model, but some type of vehicle that Max wasn't familiar with.

The driver stared Max down as he drove slowly by.

Max only noticed that he was holding his breath until the truck passed. He watched it in his rearview mirror. With that kind of fire power, they could riddle his Jeep with bullet holes in seconds, killing him instantly. His Glock wouldn't do anything against that, obviously.

It was only a matter of time before the authorities

became splintered, fractioning off into their own groups, looking out for their own survival. And they would be the ones with the guns. Or they would fall prey to others who wanted their weapons. Either way, Max simply wasn't equipped to fight off people with huge guns like that. His Glock was certainly not going to be a match for well-trained police officers and soldiers with automatic rifles.

Max took a deep breath as he parked his Jeep. He knew what he had to do. He had to get into his apartment, get his supplies, gather all the food and water that he could, and high tail it on out of this town.

He didn't know if the roads would be blocked. He hadn't planned on that before, that a serious curfew type situation might be implemented. But seeing the cop and the soldiers, his mind was starting to change.

Better to get out as soon as possible, before things got really bad.

The lights in all the apartment buildings were off, of course. There were four apartment buildings that faced the parking lot, which sat in the middle, like a kind of courtyard.

He used his small pocket LED flashlight as he walked into his apartment. It was clean and tidy, but not overly so, not that you'd be able to tell without the lights on. Not much light ever came in through the windows, and today was no exception.

There was his pull up bar, in the doorway, and there were his weights stacked neatly against the wall. He was glad now that he'd put in all that work. But would it be enough? Would his body be able to sustain the rigors of the journey ahead?

Max moved quickly through his apartment. It was a small unit, exactly the same as all the apartments in the building. He had a bedroom, a living room, and a small kitchen.

Max didn't feel sentimental at all about leaving things behind. He grabbed what he needed. In the kitchen, he methodically yet quickly took every piece of food and put it into paper bags, which were the only bags he could find. He'd worry about what might spoil later. Fortunately, most of what he had were canned goods, rice, sugar, that sort of thing.

His camping stove, with extra fuel containers, was already in his bug out bag. He cursed himself again for not completing the bag.

It was sitting in the corner of his bedroom, looking tidy. Tidy, but not yet complete. There wasn't a single mark on the bag. He'd bought it new at the store, and had never used it. He'd never even so much as been camping or hiking in the last few years.

Yeah, he was seriously lacking in a lot of areas.

As Max gathered the possessions he would need, he didn't hear a single sound from the neighbors. Everything sounded deathly quiet. The background noise of the cars was simply absent, as it had been since the EMP. It was funny that he'd never noticed the background noise before.

Max took trips out to his Jeep without seeing anyone, his arms loaded down with paper bags full of food.

Next, he brought out his bag, which contained the camping stove, the water purifier tablets, the first aid kit, the compass, etc.

Maps... shit...

The thought suddenly hit him. He didn't have any maps.

He'd been meaning to buy them for months now. But he'd always put it off. That was part of the malaise he'd been feeling. He didn't think it had been depression, but more like a general discontentment with the way things were going. He'd been motivated in some area—doing his exercises daily, for instance. But he'd slacked off severely in other areas.

Like buying maps.

Whatever, he'd just have to work it out along the way. How hard could it be, anyway? He mostly remembered the route. Something like take 476 N, obviously, and then basically head west at some point... He didn't remember exactly where.

Some roads might be blocked off. Some might be impassable. That was where the maps were going to come in.

Max cursed himself again.

But he had to keep moving. He had to keep preparing. He checked his watch, and decided he wanted to be out of there in fifteen minutes. Max's watch was a purely mechanical analog watch, winding itself from the movements of Max's wrist. It had cost a pretty penny, but in situations like this, it was worth it, although truthfully Max didn't know if regular digital watches would continue to work or not.

Max kept his flashlight on the lowest setting to conserve its battery. When he didn't absolutely need it, he hit the button to turn it off. He would be able to use this battery, and his four spares, before his flashlight became nothing but an obsolete metal cylinder. Possibly never to work again.

Society might fall completely apart. It might not. It might rebuild itself. All Max knew was that he wanted to be far, far away from everything when people were figuring out whether or not they were going to kill each other and fall into chaos, or work together to rebuild.

Frankly, Max didn't have high hopes for humanity. He'd seen the way people were these days. He'd seen them in the super market aisles screaming at each other over petty disagreements. He'd seen the news, seen people shooting each other over nothing. Husbands were murdering wives and wives were murdering their children. The world wasn't the same as it had been, and it was clearly sinking into some awful state from which it might never return. The EMP might just be the final nail in the coffin, the event that pushed everything and everyone completely over the edge once and for all.

Max had finished his last pass of his apartment. He didn't even look behind him into his old apartment. It wasn't like there had been a lot of happy memories there. Max had nothing there that he wanted to take with him. Well, maybe the pictures of his parents.

But if he couldn't eat it or shoot it, or use it in a similar way, it had to stay behind.

He was in the lobby outside his apartment door, heading towards his car. He still hadn't run into any of the neighbors. That was probably for the best. He didn't want to be forced to take anyone with him. Not that he would. This was the time for hard decisions, and Max was ready to make them. He only had enough food for himself.

"Help!" screamed someone, a female voice, shrill and terrified.

The sound was clearly coming from his neighbor's apartment across the lobby. Mandy and Ted had moved in about a year ago, but Max hadn't seen much of them. He liked to keep to himself, anyway. Ted had moved out last week, during a huge screaming battle between the two of them. It wasn't Max's business, so he'd just turned up the volume on his music player as he did his exercises.

Max paused, his arms full of two paper bags of the last of the kitchen goods.

She screamed again. It was one of the most haunting sounds Max had ever heard in his life.

Adrenalin started coursing through him.

His gaze was fixed on Mandy's closed door. Who knew what kind of horrors were going on behind it.

This was it. This was the start.

Was Max going to do the practical thing and leave, ignoring her cries for help? Was he going to save himself or attempt to help a woman he barely knew? Was he going to risk his life getting involved in a situation he knew nothing about?

Max indistinctly knew there'd be more situations like this. He'd have to make this decision time and time again on his journey. Which leg was he going to start off on?

His breathing was ragged and his heart was pounding as he stared at her door, the paper bags still clutched in his arms.

4

MANDY

Mandy had been sitting on her sofa, contemplating her headache and the strange military truck that had disappeared, when two men had kicked down her back door.

They must have climbed up the fire escape.

Mandy had screamed as loud as she could.

But they rushed over to her and the big one pointed a pistol right into her mouth, jamming the cold steel muzzle of the gun into her.

"Say another word and you're dead," he mumbled at her. He sounded drunk or high. He was big, built like a bodybuilder.

Her thoughts were racing, but they weren't clear. Everything seemed to be happening too fast. Her body felt cold, freezing cold with the fear of death.

The other man was overweight, with a huge belly and something like an overly exaggerated bad posture. He had a pistol in his hand too.

Neither wore masks.

Mandy couldn't help it. She screamed once more.

"Screw you," growled the man with the pistol, hitting her hard in the head with his other hand, formed into a fist.

The blow hurt, but didn't knock her out. Her vision went blurry, but she managed to fix her eyes right on him. She had a strange thought circling her head—she wanted to memorize his face. Whatever he was going to do to her, she wanted to know who he was, and she wanted him to know that she knew.

She couldn't believe the audacity of these men, coming in without masks. She'd be able to identify them to the police later for sure. Unless they killed her. Maybe that was what they planned to do. Maybe the gun wasn't a meaningless threat. Maybe they were going to rape her and kill her.

Mandy's heart was beating like it was about to explode out of her chest.

"Ready for some fun?" muttered the bodybuilding type guy to his friend.

The friend walked closer and leered at Mandy. His face was a blur to Mandy, but she saw that he had a fat face and a small nose. She couldn't make out the rest of it. The man with the gun in her mouth had sharp features and a long nose, and short, military-style hair.

"You go first, man," growled the bodybuilder. "I want to watch."

"You're a sick man," said the other.

Mandy made a noise, which was hard to do with the gun in her mouth.

"Don't worry, honey, we'll *take care of you*. And don't worry about the cops, they're busy..."

The other chuckled. "Everything's turned off. And who knows when it's going to be back on. We're going to have some fun while we can."

The fat one started undoing his belt. To do so, he put his gun down on the coffee table.

"Trust me, you're going to like it. We've been watching your stuck up ass every day when you come home from work…"

They'd been watching her? They knew where she lived? This wasn't just a random attack?

And they were doing all this just because the power was out? None of this made any sense to Mandy. If they had been watching her, that must mean that they were local. Surely they would know that Mandy would turn them over to the cops at the first opportunity.

She tried to calm herself down. She didn't want to be raped, but she didn't want to die more.

Suddenly, there was a noise at the door, as if someone was kicking it.

"Shit," said one of the men.

"Don't worry about it. Just some noisy neighbor."

"Don't you make a damn sound," said the one with the gun in her mouth. "Don't worry, this'll be more fun if you're alive. But it's not strictly necessary."

Who were these sick monsters?

Another sound at the door. Then another.

Was someone coming to rescue her?

She didn't know who it could possibly be. Surely it wouldn't be Mrs. Kerns, trying to kick down her door, having placed her cane carefully against the wall in the hallway.

The door burst open. She saw the flash of a foot wearing a boot. But no one stepped through the door.

The man who had unbuckled his belt and undone his fly reached slowly for his gun on the coffee table.

5

GEORGIA

G eorgia was a thin woman in her late forties, raising two kids on her own without a man in the house. But she wouldn't let anyone give her that "I'm a struggling single mother" line of crap. She didn't take shit, but she could sure dish it out when she needed to.

Her husband had left her ten years ago, and she was glad to be rid of him. She'd been the one who'd had to fix everything around the house. She'd been the one to mow the lawn and give the mechanic hell when he was ripping them off.

She didn't fit into the suburban culture where she lived. It didn't drive her crazy, since she could get away on hunting trips when she needed to. She was here because the school system was the best in the state. Her kids needed a good education.

She could hold her own in a drinking contest or on the shooting range. Out hunting deer, she was almost scary— the way she always worked with precision and dedication, no matter what. One moment, she'd be telling her hunting buddies the raunchiest joke imaginable, sipping from a tall boy, and the next, she'd spotted the deer, and then suddenly she was all business. The jokes would fall to the side, and she'd get the animal in her crosshairs, controlling her breath as she pulled the trigger.

Georgia knew something wasn't right. She drove a beat up pickup around town, and the police radio scanner had gone dead. People asked her why she carted that scanner around with her, and she'd never give a straight answer. Maybe she'd been expecting something for a while. Maybe she'd had an inkling that things hadn't been right for some time. Everything just seemed so fragile—the whole system. Maybe she herself didn't exactly have the answer.

The important thing was that she had it, and now it was dead.

The regular radio didn't work either.

The traffic lights weren't working. There weren't any cops around. She drove slowly along the four lane road, peering into the businesses she passed. There weren't any lights on inside either.

Georgia worked a collection of odd jobs. It suited her. She'd never liked to be in one place too long. She didn't like the feeling of being stationary. One of her jobs was delivering food to the rich folks around these parts. She would never fit into an office setting, and the delivery business suited her in other ways too. She also did some shifts as a bartender, when the mood struck her.

She had the hotbag in the backseat, and she was already five minutes late for the delivery. She was supposed to go right to the residential house and hand over the plate of pasta, or whatever it was, and head back to the store.

But Georgia wasn't going to do that.

She knew how to trust her instincts.

Even though no one else she could see was acting

freaked out, she knew to trust herself. She knew, for instance, before picking it up, that her cell phone wouldn't work.

She made a quick and very illegal U-turn in the middle of the road. A couple cars honked at her.

She downshifted and jammed her foot on the accelerator. If something was going on, her first priority was protecting her kids. Right now they were in school, where surely the teachers were feeding them some bullshit line about everything being fine.

Georgia drove her pickup right up to the front of the school. Both her kids were in high school and thankfully both were in the same building, so she wouldn't have to go to two separate schools.

The doors were unlocked. Probably the computerized mechanism that controlled them had simply gone dead. Georgia didn't pay the security notices any mind and simply walked into the building.

"May I help you?" called out the secretary.

"No," replied Georgia, swinging her head around to address the secretary in the briefest way possible. Her long blonde ponytail swung with her.

People often gave her admiring comments about how much energy she had. The implication was that she was too old to be doing everything that she did. She had never paid her age any mind. She simply gave it no thought. That was the way she'd dealt with a lot of her life. Her motto was that it was often easier to simply go on living than to spend too much time worrying about something you couldn't control. She knew she couldn't control the years creeping up on her, so she didn't worry about it.

She walked at a brisk pace to where James had his math class. Fortunately, she knew her kids' schedules by heart. The reason was a little unfortunate. They were known for trying to cut class as much as possible. Sometimes they didn't even go to school, and Georgia would find them hiding in their rooms by the time class had already started. Sometimes she didn't find them until she stopped at home on her lunch break. She'd just grab them by their collars and drag them into her truck, and then drop them off at the appropriate classroom. The principal had asked to speak to her about it, but she hadn't paid that any mind. She wasn't big on meetings, to say the least. She wasn't big on rules either, and she certainly hadn't been the most diligent student in her day. Instead of going to class, she'd be out back smoking cigarettes with the bad kids. But despite her lack of regrets, she knew that there were some footsteps of hers that her kids did not need to follow in.

"James!" she called, opening the door.

Twenty teenagers stared back at her. The room was darkened. The blinds were open, to let in some of the natural light.

"Excuse me," said the teacher. "What are you doing here? Do you have a pass?" He was a man in his early twenties, who clearly thought he was king of the world, not to mention his classroom.

James put his head down. He looked the epitome of embarrassment.

"James, come on. There's been an emergency."

James got up slowly from his desk. All of the other students stared back and forth between Georgia and James.

"Do you have a pass?" said the teacher.

Georgia just ignored him.

She grabbed James's hand.

"Mom!" whispered James, in the hallway. "What are you

doing? You can't just come barging into my classroom like that."

"Is your sister in English right now?" For some reason, Georgia was second guessing herself on her daughter's schedule.

"Yeah," said James. "Mom, what the hell are you doing?"

"Just come with me. You don't like school, right? You're always trying to skip it. Now your mother's taking you out of school. What do you think of that?"

James shrugged, but his mood seemed to change. "She's down here," said James, pointing down a dark hallway.

Georgia did the same thing in Sadie's classroom, opening the door, ignoring the teacher, and demanding that Sadie follow her.

Under the sunny sky, they all piled into the front seat of the beat up pickup.

"Smells good," said James, eyeing the hot bag in the small back seats.

"Would someone please tell me what in the world is going on? Why did you take us out of school, Mom?"

"Something's happening," said Georgia. "We're going to..."

She paused, realizing that she didn't know what to do next.

Around her, there were no outward signs that anything was wrong. In fact, while it had been off and on again cloudy all day, the sun was now shining brightly. The trees and grass had never looked more beautiful. No one was running around like chickens with their heads cut off. No one was rioting.

But she knew. Georgia knew.

She made a snap decision.

"We're going on a little trip," she said.

"What?" said Sadie.

"Yeah," said James. "What the hell, Mom?"

"Watch your language, James," said Georgia. "Something's not right... We're going to take a little trip up to your grandfather's old hunting cabin."

"What?" said Sadie, her voice rising in extreme disbelief.

"Something's happening," said Georgia. "Didn't you notice that nothing's working? None of the machines."

"We get it," said James. "You don't like machines, Mom. You never have. That doesn't mean the world's ending..." He instinctively pulled out his smartphone. Like so many teenagers, he seemed to live on it.

His sister Sadie did the same thing.

Of course, both phones were completely dead.

"I don't get it," whined Sadie. "It had a full charge."

Georgia wasn't going to waste time convincing them one way or the other. In fact, she wasn't sure of much these days.

She only knew to trust her instincts, and that was what she was going to do now.

"You two should be happy," said Georgia. "You won't have to go to school. We can lay low up there for a few weeks."

"Weeks?" said Sadie. "I can't miss two weeks of school..."

"You almost never go," said James, interrupting her.

"Yeah," said Georgia. "I thought you'd love a chance to miss school."

"It's John," said James, teasing his sister. "She's got a new boyfriend."

"I do not," said Sadie.

Georgia let them argue amongst themselves. Her mind, at the moment, was on other things altogether. Her plan was to get home and grab the camping gear and her rifles, as well as some food. Then they'd hit the roads as soon as they could. She had a very bad feeling. It was like a tightness in her chest. And she wasn't the type to get anxious.

Georgia kept her thoughts to herself, as she didn't want to worry her kids too much... not yet, anyway. If something bad had really happened, would Georgia really be able to keep her family alive? She could hunt. She could fish. She knew some edible plants. But would that be enough? Georgia had spent enough time in the woods to know that there was more to surviving than just eating.

6

MAX

Max had made possibly the worst decision of his life.

He'd told himself he wouldn't get involved. He'd known right from the beginning that there would be situations like this, but he'd promised himself that he needed to look out for himself.

He didn't even know Mandy and he didn't even know if it was her in the apartment.

The door had broken off its hinges completely. It was a cheap one, with a cheap frame, and even worse were the screws, which must have been so short they barely went into the wood.

Max waited, standing just out of sight in the lobby.

He took a deep breath, like he'd practiced at the range. He felt surprisingly calm. His hands weren't shaking, and his mind was clear and practical. He knew there was a host of unknowns waiting for him in that apartment. And he knew that his time to get out of town was severely limited, and this was only taking up more of it.

The adrenaline was coursing through him, making him

feel energized and cold. He felt like he could take everyone on at once in that moment. But he had enough sense to know that that wasn't true. It he simply ran into the room, he might be shot down.

But he had to enter at some point.

He stuck his Glock around the corner. His finger was inside the trigger guard. What a weird feeling, to be away from the gun range with his finger in the trigger guard. Normally, he followed strict gun safety.

He poked his head around slowly.

He took in the scene instantly. Mandy was on the couch, a gun in her mouth. Two armed men were there. One athletic, one not. Not that that would even matter.

To Max's surprise, the fat one with the gun in Mandy's mouth chuckled as Max peered into the room, leaving as much of his body as possible hidden behind the doorframe.

The other man pointed his gun right at Max. It was a pistol, one of those cheap numbers made who knows where. It might jam at any moment, not that Max could count on that for his own safety.

Mandy's eyes turned towards him, a pleading look in them. But there was hope too.

"You know the deal," mumbled the fat one loudly. "Come in and we shoot her. Not that it makes much difference to us."

"Or join us for the fun," said the other one.

They spoke strangely, as if they were on drugs.

How disgusting. They were only a couple hours out from the EMP, and already these sickos were breaking into homes to rape vulnerable women. The majority of Max's colleagues were probably still at work. Society was likely divided—the people who didn't know what was going on and were simply waiting for the power to come back on, and the people who had been lurking in the shadows just waiting for an opportunity like this to cut loose and do what they'd always wanted to do, which was cause chaos and have their fun.

And then there were the people like Max. He knew he didn't fit into either of the other categories. But he wasn't sure what category he *was* in. He'd thought of himself as a prepper, or at least a practical person with some measures in place in case shit hit the fan. Now he wasn't so sure. He hadn't planned on coming across two armed men so early.

The fat man had mumbled like he was on drugs. Max didn't think he was drunk. But he couldn't identify what drug he might be on. Maybe one of those new synthetic designer drugs shipped from China, the ones with devastating and strange effects on the mind and body.

"Drop the guns," said Max, loudly and clearly.

But as he said it, he knew they wouldn't do it. There was no reasoning with these animals.

The fat man moved first. Everything seemed to slow down, but in reality it all happened very quickly.

Max shot first, before the fat man could even squeeze the trigger.

Max hit him in the forehead. He crumpled instantly.

The man with the gun in Mandy's mouth froze. He didn't seem to know what to do. He watched with a horrified expression as his friend fell.

"One more... move," he mumbled loudly. His eyes looked crazy, his pupils wide. "One more move... I'll shoot her. I will..."

Max aimed carefully at the man. He knew he could take him out first. He squeezed the trigger, the bullet hitting the man in the chest. He crumpled, his weight falling onto Mandy.

She let out a long scream, muffled by the gun still in her mouth.

Max rushed over. He seized the dead man around the waist and pulled with all his might. The guy was huge, and it took all of Max's effort to pull the body off her.

"Is anyone else here?" said Max.

Mandy was sobbing, tears rolling down her face rapidly.

She shook her head, but didn't seem to be able to speak.

"It's OK," said Max, automatically offering words of consolation. But they sounded hollow even to him. In fact, he knew that everything was decidedly not OK. This was just the beginning.

"What's going on?" she said, sobbing.

Max didn't know what to do. He'd never been good at comforting crying women. Fortunately for him, there wasn't time for that anyway.

But he had to think fast. Was he going to leave her here? He had to get on with his own plan. He'd made this little pit stop and saved her life. Wasn't that enough?

Max knew that it was every man and woman for themselves at this point. He had drilled it into his head a thousand times, but he'd already made a grave mistake. A little too far along this path and there would be no turning back. He'd be taking care of whole families.

Max checked his watch. Twenty minutes had gone by. It might already be too late. People surely would be realizing by now that it wasn't just the power. They'd start panicking. Who knew what would happen next.

If there was one thing Max had learned in his hours of internet research, it was that no one really knew what was going to happen when the shit hit the fan.

It had hit, and it was about to splatter everywhere.

"What's going on?" she said again. "What's happening? Who were those men?"

Max took a good look at her. He hadn't really gotten one earlier, with all the commotion.

The bodies were still on the floor, but strangely they didn't affect Max in the slightest. He'd had his little episode of brief panic in the darkened stairwell after work, but he seemed to have gotten over it quickly enough. His mind was set on his mission, on achieving the objectives that he knew (or hoped) would be crucial to his survival.

She was an attractive woman in her twenties. She was thin, but had the kind of womanly figure that Max liked—a full figure, with hips, a good ass, a large chest. She had long dark hair that hung down her shoulders. A woman of the old style, nothing odd about her. No tattoos, no extravagant makeup. She looked fit and healthy.

Max sat down on the couch next to her.

"Listen," he said. "There's a lot going on." He didn't bother trying to make his voice soothing. There wasn't time for that now, and he knew it. "Things have changed, and they might never go back to how they were before."

"What are you talking about?" she said.

"It's not just the power," said Max. "Everything's going to be gone. People are going to be... well, you saw how they acted."

She didn't seem to be catching his drift. "They're animals," she said, carefully avoiding looking at the corpses. "I can't believe it... I just can't... Shouldn't we call the police or something?"

"The phones won't work," said Max. "Nothing works. And it might never work again. Listen, this is important. This could be the start of the breakdown of our modern society. One event like this... I think it must have been an

EMP. If it was a coronal event or some kind of weapon... I have no way of knowing..."

"We've got to call the police!" she said, almost hysterical.

"Do you have food? Water? Do you have a firearm?" Max's mind was jumping right to the practical. If he was going to leave her here, he wanted to know that she at least had a chance of surviving. She seemed like a nice girl. She didn't deserve this. But then again, not many did. No one deserved to see their society come crumbling down around their feet while they starved to death and fought tooth and nail for the last morsel of food.

"What?" she said. "What are you talking about? You just shot two men... I mean, I know it was justified, but... aren't you worried?"

"Worried?" said Max, momentarily confused. "Look, you've got to understand what's happening, for your own safety. Unfortunately, there isn't much time. There was some kind of EMP..."

"EMP?"

Max sighed.

But at least she'd stopped crying. And at least she was somewhat listening to him now. She seemed more 'with it.'

Finally, Max had the bright idea of taking her into the kitchen, away from the bodies. They seemed to be bothering her much more than they bothered him, which wasn't much at all.

Not that he'd ever seen a real dead body before. It wasn't that unusual for someone to go their whole adult life without ever seeing a dead person. That was what modern society did, it took the normal things of life and sheltered everyone from them. Death was for morticians to deal with, for EMTs, for doctors, not for regular people. Everyone was sheltered, and that was going to come bite them in the ass.

"Look," said Max. "What you need to know is that the power's out, on all devices, and it's not going to come back in. You can tell something's different, right?"

She nodded.

Now she was listening. And she seemed to think Max knew what he was talking about, because she was listening very carefully.

"So what do we do?" she said.

Max didn't say anything for a moment.

He wasn't really thinking. He said it automatically. And as soon as he said it, he instantly regretted it.

"Come with me," he said. "I have an old farmhouse... inherited. I'm getting out of here. People are going to become animals. You already saw it."

Why was he trying to convince her to come with him? Was he crazy? She'd slow him down. He couldn't bring everyone he met alone the way with him to safety. And he hadn't even left his apartment building yet.

"Come with you?" she said, mulling the words over as she said them. There was that pensive look in her eyes.

"Yeah," said Max. "I'm getting out of here. I mean, think about it. The shipping systems are gone. There isn't going to be food. You saw those animals in there." He gestured into the room with the two bodies.

She shuddered at the thought.

Damnit, thought Max to himself. Here he was, being too soft. Really, what good would she do him in the woods, out on the road? She couldn't even stomach the sight of some bodies.

"There was a truck..." she said slowly.

"A truck?" said Max, confused.

Meanwhile, all he could think about was getting out of there and getting on the road.

But for some reason he stayed. He didn't know why, and maybe he never would.

Maybe there was something about her. But this wasn't a damn love story and Max knew it.

"Yeah," she said. "Some kind of military truck. I saw it with Mrs. Kerns, you know the neighbor... It was huge, with this big gun on the back... it circled slowly around the parking lot. It was really eerie. And the weird thing... It didn't have any US markings on it."

"No markings on it?" said Max, worried. "Are you sure?"

She shrugged. "I'm not sure."

Max pondered this for a moment.

"I saw a truck like that coming in," he said. "But I'm pretty sure I saw US markings on it. I thought it was the army... I figured they'd been dispatched. What I think will happen is that the police and army will put up roadblocks pretty soon. They'll start clamping down, imposing a curfew. But meanwhile, communications will never come for them. Supplies will never come. They'll be confused just like the general population... It'll devolve quickly after that. There's only so long you can keep the chaos at bay, even for the military..."

"Shit," muttered Mandy. "Shit, shit, shit...."

"What?" said Max.

"There are two guys dead in my living room... And you're telling me the world is ending... I really should have gone to work today."

She was freaking out.

Max looked at his watch. "Look," he said. "I shouldn't even be telling you to come with me. Here's the deal. I've got to leave now. Are you coming with me or not?"

Mandy didn't say anything for a moment. She seemed to be studying his face. Max had gotten this look before. He'd noticed that cops and people like that had a way of studying your face to tell whether or not you were full of shit. Mandy had that way of looking at him.

Maybe there was more to her than met the eye. She could be useful after all.

"OK," she said.

"OK?"

"I'll come."

Max nodded. "OK," he said. "Let's get to work. What supplies do you have?"

"Supplies?"

"Food, candles, flashlights, knives, guns..."

She laughed nervously. "I've never even touched a gun," she said.

Max groaned internally, but he pushed through it. This wasn't the time for ideology. It was the time for being practical.

"OK," he said. "Get everything else that might be useful. Nothing electronic. Do a quick sweep of the apartment. Five minutes, OK? You've got five minutes. I'll hit the kitchen and grab all the food. You know where the other things are. Remember: you're looking for flashlights..."

"I got it," said Mandy.

Max was surprised to see her move quickly and rapidly. She went right into the bedroom, and he watched her for a moment through the doorway. She moved efficiently through the drawers.

Max looked around the kitchen. It was a mess. But there was food.

He did the refrigerator first, then the freezer. They could eat the perishable goods first, and then move on to the canned things.

He found a huge bag of stale rice under the sink, as well

as a huge pot roast in the freezer. It had freezer burn on it, but that didn't matter. Mandy actually had quite a few cans of beef soup, and Max made a couple trips down to his Jeep to stock up.

Outside in the parking lot, the light from the day was already getting low. This little incident with Mandy had taken more time than he'd realized. Of course, the lights were off everywhere, in every building. Max wondered briefly about home generators, and whether or not they would work. But it didn't matter.

Even though the sun was still partially in the sky, the town looked darker than Max had ever seen it. There was no light pollution. He'd have to get used to this.

"OK," said Mandy, appearing by his side with a couple duffel bags. "I think I got some good stuff."

Max nodded at her.

"Let's go," he said, stuffing the bags into the back seat. The Jeep was almost full at this point.

"Wait," said Mandy. "There's Mrs. Kerns... What's she going to do?"

"She'll be fine," muttered Max. He knew that she wouldn't be fine, but there wasn't anything he could do about it.

He looked at Mrs. Kerns. He'd seen her before, and spoken to her briefly. It wasn't her age that made him make the decision—for one thing, there simply wasn't room in the Jeep. And the main thing was that she wasn't in good health. She simply wouldn't make it.

"Get in the car," said Max. "Just wave at her."

Mrs. Kerns stood unsteadily in front of the building, mouthing something at Mandy.

Max ignored her, put the Jeep into reverse, and backed up quickly.

Soon, they were out on the dark road. There were a few cars here and there, cars that seemed to move aimlessly, as if their drivers didn't know where to go or what they were doing.

"I feel so bad leaving her back there," said Mandy. "I hope she'll be OK."

Max didn't say anything.

"So," said Mandy. "How long do you think until this all boils over?"

"Boils over?"

"You know, calms down."

"It's not going to calm down," said Max. "This is it..."

"What do you mean 'this is it?'"

"I mean," said Max. "Exactly what I said. There's no turning back now."

"What?" said Mandy, sounding shocked and worried.

"Look," said Max. "People have studied this. Society isn't as robust as we'd like to think. All it takes is one event. Something just like this."

"I mean you said it would devolve... or whatever word you used. But I thought you meant things would get crazy for a couple weeks."

Max laughed. It was the first time he'd laughed in a while. He shook his head.

"It's not like that," he said. "I mean, study civilizations... past civilizations. Everything looks fine, and then something happens. The event doesn't matter. It's how people react that matters."

"You're crazy," said Mandy.

Max didn't say anything.

"Did I get in the car with some crazy guy?" she said. She sounded more like she was thinking out loud than speaking to Max.

"Look," said Max. "I don't care what you think of me. I know what I'm doing, and that's getting to this farmhouse. I want to be as far away from large groups of people as I can. There're the real danger. You don't want to be around them. Either come with me, or get out right now. I don't want to take you halfway there. It'll be too late, and I'm not turning around."

She didn't say anything for a moment.

"I know you're not crazy," she said quietly. "I saw it in your face."

That sounded like some hippie bullshit to Max, but he'd seen the way she'd studied him. There was something to it. She could read people, and she was intuitive. That might be valuable when paired with Max's more practical skills. Although, now that he started thinking about it, he might not be so useful after all. When was the last time he'd started a fire in the woods, or hunted game? He remembered going hunting once as a kid, and he didn't shoot anything. He'd just wandered around the woods for a day with his dad. His dad got drunk and Max had had to take the rifle away from him.

"So you're coming?"

"Yeah," said Mandy. "I guess I don't want to believe it... I mean, I know you're not crazy, but I'm not so sure you're right about everything collapsing... I mean, that just seems so..."

"Believe what you want," said Max. "Anyway," he added more quietly, "I hope you're right. I really do."

Max didn't want to take the highways. He didn't know what the police would be doing on them. He hadn't seen any more roadblocks like the one earlier. Who knew what was happening to the police force that had no radios and no way of communicating with themselves? Would they even be able to stay organized for a short time?

"Wow!" said Mandy loudly. "Look! That's crazy."

Max looked to where she was pointing. The night was upon them now. The sun was fully down. The night was dark, the darkest night either of them had ever seen.

They were passing by a grocery store.

Flashlights were illuminating the area. Dozens, if not hundreds, of flashlights. Not just a couple. They were shining all around haphazardly, chaotically.

"What's going on?" said Mandy. "There must be dozens of people there."

"Looting," said Max, as he surveyed the scene quickly before putting his eyes back on the road.

"Looting? Are you serious?"

The window was down, and they could hear shouting.

"You want to see?" said Max, slowing to a stop. He was about a hundred yards down the road from the store. He kept the engine idling.

He knew they had to keep moving, but he also knew it would be useful to see how people were reacting.

How would people react when the shit hit the fan? That was the big question that had been debated endlessly on internet forums.

Max knew enough to know he didn't have it *all* figured out. But he figured that different people would react differently. That is, until, the mob mentally drew them all together.

If people were already mobbing on the first night, that wasn't a good sign. Things might be devolving into chaos faster than Max had suspected. He'd figured on at least a night of good driving to get father out, away from the more densely populated areas.

"Can you see them?" said Mandy, peering into the rearview mirror. "They're acting crazy."

"Yeah," said Max. "It's happening faster than I thought."

"Maybe you're right about all this," said Mandy. "They're all yelling at once."

"Look," said Max. "A fight's breaking out."

One man was punching another. Mostly everyone was ignoring it. They were too intent on getting into the store.

"This is..."

"Crazy?" said Max.

The man getting punched went down to the ground. The big man who'd been punching him was on top of him, beating him relentlessly.

"Should we help him?" said Mandy. "No one's doing anything. He could really hurt him."

Max just shook his head and said nothing.

There was the sound of crashing glass.

The mob had broken the windows of the store. They were rushing inside.

"Didn't take long," muttered Max. "And they probably don't even realize what's happening."

"Do you think the police will come?" said Mandy.

"How would they even know? Maybe if someone's on a patrol, but who knows what's going on with the cops right now."

They could hear screaming from inside the store. The light from the flashlights was coming out in random, chaotic spurts.

The night had never seemed so dark.

Max sat there watching the outside of the building perhaps longer than he should have.

The man doing the punching had finally gotten up and rushed into the store.

"Hey," said Mandy. "There's someone running out of the store."

Max looked again.

An overweight man was springing out of the store. It was hard to see him in the darkness with the random occasional illumination from the flashlights.

"Looks like he's wearing a store uniform or something..." said Mandy.

"Maybe he's the employee," muttered Max.

A couple people jumped back through the glass and started chasing the overweight man.

"He's coming right towards us," said Mandy, alarmed.

Sure enough, she was right. The fat man was barreling towards them. He was followed by about five men, who were screaming something at him.

Suddenly, their words became clear.

"He's got the money!"

"Get him!"

"What do they want money for?" muttered Max.

"What are we going to do?" said Mandy.

"Do?" said Max. "We're leaving. That's why we're leaving. We can't help everyone. That's the breaks."

Mandy didn't say anything. Maybe she knew he was right. Or maybe she thought he was a heartless bastard. Not that it mattered much either way. The important thing now was survival, and Max knew it.

Max pushed in the clutch, put the car into first, and was about to pull away when he looked in the rearview mirror one last time.

The man was close to them, so close that Max suddenly saw his face clearly in the brake lights of the Jeep.

"Chad?" said Max.

"Chad?" said Mandy, confused.

Max didn't pull away, and the fat man was soon at the driver's window.

"You've got to help me!" he said, panting. He was completely out of breath and already covered in sweat. He couldn't have been more out of shape.

"Chad?" said Max, stunned.

He would recognize that face anywhere. He'd gone to school with Chad, and they'd been close, until they'd drifted apart. The last he'd heard, Chad was somewhere down in Miami.

"Max?" said Chad, a stunned look coming onto his face.

Shit, there was no way he could leave Chad behind. He could only imagine what that mob of animals would do to him. Chad was practically family. Sure, estranged family, but still...

Georgia couldn't blame her kids for this one. Sadie and James were trying their best to help, even though they were pretty sure their mom had gone off the deep end and gone completely crazy.

The minutes had stretched to hours, and the hours had gone by. The sun had fallen long ago.

Georgia was out in the garage of their house, with a flashlight, trying to find the last pieces of her camping gear.

It had been a while since she'd actually used the gear. Most of her recent trips had been day trips. She knew James and Sadie could fend for themselves, but now that they were older, she didn't like leaving them alone. They were more trustworthy when they were younger teens. Now they were interested in drinking, even though they were under-age, and throwing parties. Georgia knew that if she left them alone for a long weekend, she'd come back to a house completely destroyed and perhaps overrun with hungover teenagers.

"Damnit," she muttered, as she tried to push an old

kayak out of the way. It toppled down from where it was precariously perched, almost falling on her.

She stepped out of the way just in time. But there on the top shelf was what she'd been looking for—a tent. It was covered in dust that blew into the air around her as she pulled it down. It was in a nylon duffel bag. She dragged it back into the darkened kitchen that was lit with a single candle.

Sadie was at the kitchen table, staring at her dead phone.

"Staring at it won't make it turn back on," said Georgia.

"I'm waiting for a text," said Sadie.

"You're crazy," said James, entering the kitchen. "I'm beginning to think Mom's right. Something's going on, and your phone isn't going to come back on, Sadie."

"I can't deal with any more adolescent bickering right now," said Georgia. "James, help me load this into the truck."

"Here," said James, taking the tent from her and hoisting it easily over his shoulder.

She heard the front door swinging open as James left the house to drop it in the bed of the truck.

"You've got everything you need, Sadie?" said Georgia.

Sadie nodded. "I don't see why I can't take my makeup," said Sadie, pouting.

"If everything calms down, we can come back," said Georgia. "Hopefully this will just be a short trip."

"What about school?" said Sadie. "We're just going to miss two weeks of school?"

Georgia shrugged. "I'll tell them I'm homeschooling you."

Georgia was stressed, which was a relatively new feeling for her. She opened the fridge and took out the last cold beer. The rest of the beer was loaded into the truck already. She cracked it open and took a sip, savoring the flavor.

"None of this makes any sense," said Sadie. "You're talking about when things calm down, but nothing's even happened yet."

It was true, at least in Georgia's neighborhood. The other houses were completely dark, and no one seemed to be driving on the roads. There was no one out, and it gave the area an eerie feeling, like those abandoned buildings that sit tall on the horizon, rusting and rotting away, mementos to a time long gone.

Another half hour went by, and Georgia had finally gotten everything she thought they might need in the truck. She had an old map tucked between her legs, not that she needed it, since she knew the way to the cabin well. But she figured that she didn't know what was going to happen with the roads.

Sadie and James were in the truck too. Sadie sat in the front, and James was stretched out as best he could in the cramped backseat. The bed of the truck was laden down with all sorts of food and camping gear, as well as the things that Georgia hadn't been able to convince Sadie not to take. Georgia may not have taken bullshit from anyone, but she had a soft spot for her kids, and sometimes she felt like she let them get away with too much.

Georgia had just started the engine when a cop car came barreling down the road.

"Damn," muttered James from the backseat. "It's flying."

The sirens were off, but the lights were blasting through the dark night.

The cop car was a strange sight, the only thing moving in the night. Georgia didn't know where the neighbors were. Maybe they were hiding away in their houses, scared.

Who knew. She didn't have time to worry about them right now.

To her surprise, the cop car skidded to a stop right in front of her house.

Georgia waited, thinking it would be better not to drive away right now. But her instincts were telling her to just drive and not stop. She had to fight those instincts.

The cop got out of his car. His hand was on his gun in its holster. He approached the truck slowly. He bent down to lean over the windows. He was a tall man, with huge muscles.

"Street's closed," he said.

"I was just heading out to go on a camping trip with my kids," said Georgia, figuring she might as well try the diplomatic approach first.

"Sorry lady," said the cop. "No one's coming in or out."

"What's going on?"

The cop didn't answer for a moment.

Georgia was starting to get a read on him, watching his face carefully in the darkness. At first he'd seemed like one of those super stern cops. But she could see now that he wasn't like that. There was something human in his face.

"Sorry lady," he said, repeating himself. "Truth is, none of us have any idea what's going on."

"What do you mean you don't know?" said James, from the backseat. "You're the police. And you're saying you don't know what's going on."

"Everything went dead," said the cop. "As I'm sure you saw. It's not just a power outage. All I know is that I drove right to the station. So did a bunch of us. No one knew what to do without the radios. So the only thing I know is that we don't know what's going on. It was some kind of EMP."

"EMP?" said Georgia. She thought she'd heard the term

before, but she couldn't remember what it meant, or what the letters stood for.

The cop shrugged. "I don't know what it is," he said. "Something that knocks out all electrical gadgets or something. All I know is nothing works."

"Electromagnetic pulse," said James.

Georgia turned to look at him, surprised.

"I think I saw it in a movie," he said, shrugging. "What it means is that the stuff won't turn back on."

"So what's going to happen?" said Georgia, to the cop.

The cop shrugged. "Truth is, I don't know," he said. "I've been waiting for backup since the sun went down, but no one's come. The only thing I know to do is keep the road blocked like they told me. There are some other guys farther up the road, keeping all traffic from coming into the neighborhood, so you're the first people I've seen since this all happened."

"You mean they're blocking Baker Street? That's the only way into this neighborhood."

"Yeah," said the cop. "And I haven't seen anyone else."

"You mean no one else is home? All these houses are empty?"

Georgia was starting to realize that they were the only people in this entire neighborhood... Well, there might be someone at home, someone who didn't go to work, or hadn't gone to work that day. But she knew that the majority of the people around here were out of the house most of the time. It was the kind of neighborhood where people often worked two or three jobs just to keep afloat. They didn't have a ton of time to spend at home.

"So you can't let us through?" said Georgia.

"Sorry," said the cop. "Even if I did, they'd stop you on Baker Street."

"OK," said Georgia. She was thinking fast. She knew that even though this cop seemed friendly, things might take a turn for the worse if she told him she was going to disobey his orders or his advice. She respected cops a hell of a lot. They had to put up with a lot of shit. But she also knew them well. She went hunting with some of them. She knew what not to say to them. She knew how to avoid a conflict. "Thanks, officer."

The man tipped his hat. "I'll be up there at the corner if you need anything," he said. He got back in his car.

"So we're stuck here?" said Sadie, sounding terrified.

"I thought you didn't want to leave," said James.

"Quiet, kids," said Georgia. "I've got to think."

Georgia didn't panic at first. She knew there would be a way out if she needed one. She knew she had to get out, whether or not the cops wanted her to.

This might be more of an opportunity than a roadblock. If no one else was home, she could use this opportunity to take what she needed from their houses. She didn't exactly have a lot of food. James and Sadie tended to eat whatever she brought home, so it wasn't like she'd been able to stock up a lot of food.

"OK," said Georgia. "Listen carefully. This is what we're going to do. And I don't want to hear any arguing about it. We need more food if we're going..."

"I thought you were like an expert hunter," said James.

"We don't know what's going to happen. We might be in a situation where we need food and I can't hunt."

"Wait," said Sadie, divining what was going to happen. "You're suggesting we're going to break into our neighbor's houses and steal their food because they're not here?"

"That's exactly what I'm suggesting," said Georgia. "Except that I'm not suggesting it. That's what's going to happen. Period. My priority is protecting you two, and that involves feeding you. And for all we know, our neighbors may never get home. Who knows what's going to happen with the road block."

"Cool," said James. "I think the McKinneys have a ton of food in their basement."

"OK," said Georgia. "We'll start there. We'll fill up the truck. Everything we can possibly carry. And then we'll get out of here."

"Sounds cool, Mom," said James, apparently impressed with his mother's criminal inclinations. "But how are we going to get past the cops?"

"We'll think of something," said Georgia. She thought of her rifles. She didn't want to use them. She'd never shot anything other than an animal. But if people were turning into animals, maybe she'd have to do what she had to do... But shooting a cop? There was no way she could do that. She had too many friends on the force. And he was just an innocent guy... Then again, it was her family she was thinking about.

"Have you two lost your minds?" said Sadie, her voice shrill. "We just need to stay here. That's what the policeman said. And there's no way we can just break into the McKinneys' house..."

"Why not?" said James. "Mr. McKinney works all day managing the car wash. There's no way he's home. Charlotte's at school. She's in my math class. And Mrs. McKinney works today."

"How do you know their whole schedule?" said Georgia. James didn't say anything.

"Because he spies on Mrs. McKinney taking a shower."

"Gross, James," said Georgia, chuckling to herself.

"I do not," said James.

"I caught you doing it," said Sadie.

"I don't want to hear any more," said Georgia. "And I mean that. Now here's what's going to happen. James, you and me are going to head inside. Sadie, you stay in the truck."

"I want to go back in our house," whined Sadie.

"End of discussion," said Georgia.

She killed the truck engine. She should have turned it off earlier to save gas, but her mind had been turned to other things.

She and James got out of the truck. Sadie sat in the front seat with her arms crossed.

Georgia grabbed one of her rifles from the bed of the truck. She considered handing one to Sadie for a moment, but realized that the chances were higher that Sadie would accidentally hurt herself with it rather than use it to defend herself. She cursed herself for not taking Sadie to the shooting range. She'd taken James, who'd been eager to learn. Georgia had figured that there'd be time to convince Sadie to learn. Now it was too late. Sadie would have to learn on the road, when it was necessary. She'd have to get over her prissy ways and learn to do what she had to do.

"Don't I need a gun?" said James.

Georgia shook her head. "I'll carry the gun," she said. "You're going to be carrying supplies."

James grumbled, but he did what she said, and he followed her into the McKinneys' backyard.

"It's so dark," whispered James.

Georgia took out her flashlight. James had one too. But it was still dark. The lights from the flashlights were just thin pale beams fighting against the incredible darkness of a night without any power for miles and miles. For all Georgia knew, the whole country was like this. Without communication, there was no way to know.

"I don't think anyone's home," whispered James.

"I know," whispered Georgia. "Let's not get into how you know their schedule."

If it wasn't so dark, Georgia was pretty sure that she'd be able to see him blushing.

The backyard had hedges that lined it. Georgia couldn't see the pickup, and she was worried about Sadie, even though supposedly no one was in the area.

"Let's make this quick," whispered Georgia. "Just follow me. It'd be better if we don't speak much."

"Why? There's no one here."

"Shh," whispered Georgia.

The house would be easy to break into. The kitchen faced the back, and there were huge windows that lined the wall, along with a sliding glass door.

Georgia peered inside. Sure enough, there wasn't a spark of light. Not even a candle flickering far off. Likely, there wasn't anyone home. She was friendly with the McKinneys, and she would have expected them to come over and ask what was going on with the power.

Georgia tried the sliding door without luck. It was locked.

They tried a window. That was locked too.

So she took the butt of her rifle and slammed it into the glass.

"Way to go, Mom," whispered James. "Badass."

"Shh," said Georgia, as she stuck her hand carefully through the broken glass.

She lifted the window open.

"I'm going first," she whispered.

It took some effort, but the window was large, and she

could climb through it easily. The broken glass wasn't a danger, since she'd simply slid the window open.

She shone her flashlight around, looking for signs of life. Nothing. She walked over to the sliding glass door and unlatched it, so that James could come in. She slid open the heavy door, and gestured for James to follow her.

But he didn't move. He was standing frozen.

"James," she hissed. "Come on."

James didn't respond. In fact, he didn't move a muscle, not even when Georgia shone her flashlight beam directly on him. She put the beam on his face, and saw the expression of extreme fear there.

"Put the gun down slowly," came a male voice. "Or your son is getting shot."

"Mark?" said Georgia, surprised.

It was Mark McKinney, head of the household.

"I thought you were supposed to be at work."

"Change of plans," said Mark.

Georgia couldn't see him. He was just a disembodied voice.

"So you came over to rob us," said Mark McKinney.

"No," said Georgia, keeping the gun in her hand. Mark didn't have a flashlight, and he figured he wouldn't be able to see her clearly, or see whether or not she'd put the gun down. He also didn't seem too good at this: he'd told her to put the gun down, and then spoken to her anyway. "We came over to see if you were OK."

"Lies," said Mark. "I heard everything. I heard you talking in your truck. Like you said, it's either your family or mine. And I'm not going to let you rob us. Now put the gun down like I said."

Suddenly, Mark turned on a lantern that he'd had outside. The whole area became dimly illuminated.

He could see her and Georgia could see him.

He wore a grim expression on his face, and he pointed a .45 directly at James's stomach.

"Let's calm down," said Georgia in a low voice.

"I'm not calming down until you drop that rifle."

James didn't move a muscle, but his eyes turned to Georgia. There was a pleading, terrified look to them.

8

MANDY

"They're coming!" screamed Mandy. "Go! Go! I thought you were going to go!"

"We can't leave him," said Max. He was looking at this guy who was supposedly named Chad.

"But they're coming!"

Mandy was watching them in the rearview mirror. They were sprinting as fast as they could towards the car.

Chad was standing at the driver's side window, panting, covered in sweat. He looked like a mess. His hair was matted and drenched. His employee golf shirt was ruffled, like he'd been grabbed.

Mandy didn't understand what was going on. Max had been dead set on leaving them all behind and just going. Now the roles were reversed, and Mandy knew they needed to get out of there.

"Chad?" said Max. "Chad?"

But Chad didn't respond. He didn't say anything. He looked like he might have been in shock, or maybe on drugs. He had that glazed look on his face, like he didn't really know what was going on.

Max opened his door and got out.

"What are you doing?" screamed Mandy.

The people rushing towards them were getting closer. Two of them had something in their hands, baseball bats, sticks, or rudimentary clubs. She couldn't tell. But the way they were running terrified her. They'd already turned into animals.

Max had been right—they needed to *leave*.

"Come on, Chad," said Max, grabbing his friend and shaking him. "Wake the hell up."

Chad didn't respond. He just gazed at Max vaguely. There wasn't a spark of recognition on his face.

If there was anybody that should be left behind, thought Mandy, it was this guy Chad. What good would he do them? What purpose would he serve them?

Max opened the door to the backseat and started grabbing bags and supplies and throwing them onto the road.

"We need those!" screamed Mandy.

"He's too big to put in the front seat with you," yelled Max.

He slammed his body into the wall of supplies and stuff that was piled high in the backseat. He pushed his body against it, trying to cram everything into a tighter order so that it wouldn't take up so much space.

"Come on, Chad, buddy," said Max, trying to push the big man into the Jeep.

"They're coming!"

The men weren't far away at all. She could clearly see one waving a metal baseball bat wildly. His face looked insane—pure animalistic anger.

Mandy couldn't believe it was all coming true. Society really was already falling into complete chaos.

"There you go, Chad," said Max, slamming his weight

against his big friend in the backseat. Finally, Chad was in. Max slammed the door and hopped into the driver's seat quickly.

"Go!" shouted Mandy.

Max didn't hesitate for a single second. He jammed the car into gear and they were off. He didn't even bother closing his door. He simply let the acceleration of the car close the door for him.

The crazy men were only a few feet away. Mandy thought maybe one of them had touched the bumper.

She watched them in the mirror, disappearing as Max, Mandy, and Chad sped away.

Something hit the back of the car, making a small crack in the rear windshield.

"Someone threw a baseball bat," said Max.

"Do you want to tell me what that was all about?" said Mandy, looking at Max. Now she looked at Chad in the backseat. Now that he was in the car, she could smell him. He stunk of potent weed mixed with sweat. It wasn't a good smell. He stared blankly at the headrest in front of him. He was still panting.

"He's an old friend," said Max, not looking back at Chad. "He must be shocked. We barely got him away from those animals."

"And stoned," added Mandy.

"Probably," said Max. "He always had a bit of a problem with substances..."

"So you thought you'd risk our lives for some drug addict? What's he going to do for us?"

"I thought you were the one who was all about saving people," said Max angrily.

"I thought you were the one about being practical and ruthless."

"He's an old friend," repeated Max. "I couldn't leave him there."

"But how much of the gear did you throw out to fit him in there?"

"I don't know," said Max. "Truthfully, I don't even know what I got rid of. But I had to do it. Look, it was my decision. I'm the one bringing you along. Remember where you'd be without me? Dead, or even worse."

"Maybe so," said Mandy. "But now that I'm here, it's no longer just you making the decisions, because it's my life on the line too."

Max started to chuckle. It surprised her.

"What does that laugher mean?" she said.

"I'm impressed," said Max. "I think you've finally realized how serious this is. And don't worry, we're not going to be making any more dangerous stops. I've already picked up two stragglers, and I'm not picking up any more."

"Good," muttered Mandy. "So what's the plan, anyway?"

"The plan," said Max, as he continued to drive into the dark night. "Is to get as far away from this area as possible. I want to drive all night. You can drive stick, right?"

"Yeah," said Mandy, although truthfully she wasn't totally sure. She'd never had a car with manual transmission, but she had driven her friend's car home once or twice from the bar. She'd gotten them home in one piece and only ground the gears a bit.

"Good," said Max. "I'll need to sleep at some point, and then you can drive. But I'll drive now. I have no idea what we're going to encounter. If we run into trouble, I'm prepared for it."

He lifted his shirt to show her the gun.

"I already know you have a gun," she said sarcastically. "Remember earlier? I saw you shoot two guys with it."

Max nodded.

"So should we do something about Chad in the back?"

"We just have to wait until he's functional again," said Max.

"You mean until he sobers up."

"I guess," said Max. "When he's lucid, he's a smart guy. He might have some good ideas that could be useful for us."

"I think you're just making excuses," said Mandy. "I just don't see him as anything but a liability."

"You know I can hear you, right?" said Chad from the backseat.

Mandy was so surprised she jumped in her seat.

"I thought..."

"I may be high as a kite but I can still hear."

"How's it going, Chad?" said Max, glancing at his friend in the mirror. Not that he could see much with the darkness that seemed so pervasive, penetrating not just the car but their own bodies and thoughts.

"I'm all right," said Chad. "Thanks for grabbing me back there. I just froze up."

"I noticed," said Max.

"I'm sorry," said Mandy, turning around to speak to Chad. But she couldn't help wrinkling her nose as she smelled the full brunt of his intense stench. "I didn't mean what I said... I'm just really freaked out..."

"She your girlfriend or something?" said Chad, speaking obviously only to Max, ignoring Mandy.

"Just met her," said Max.

"Nice," said Chad, looking at Mandy, and eyeing her up and down.

"Eww," said Mandy, turning back around as Chad's eyes fell to her ample chest.

"Look, man," said Chad. "If you could update me or

something, I honestly don't know what the hell is going on. I was working the closing shift... I remember that the power went out, so I decided to just have myself a little party there in the shop... The owner is down the shore for the week, so I knew I had the place to myself... I must have passed out, because the next thing I knew, people were breaking the windows... I mean, you saw it. It was like a full fledged mob. Man, that was unreal."

"Truth is," said Max. "We don't know what's going on either. I think there was an EMP."

"Oh," said Chad, as if he knew what that meant.

"So does everyone know about these EMPs except me?" said Mandy.

"You don't know what they are?" said Chad.

"I do now," said Mandy defensively.

"So the shit's really hit the fan then?" said Chad. "Man, I've been expecting this for some time..."

"Do you have any supplies, provisions back at home?" said Max.

"Nah, man," said Chad. "I'm staying with my friend... Just crashing on his couch. I didn't have any money for stuff like that. Looks like you're pretty well equipped, though." He started poking at the pile of provisions in the seat next to him. His body was jammed up against it all, and when the car turned he had to brace himself against the weight of it all.

"Great," muttered Mandy. "At least I brought some stuff along."

"Hey man, I really appreciate this," said Chad. "So what's the plan anyway?"

"We're headed to my family's old farmhouse," said Max.

"I don't get it," said Mandy. "You two are old friends?"

"Yup," they said together.

But they couldn't have seemed more different. Max was clean cut and in shape. He didn't seem like he'd ever touched pot in his life. Chad, on the other hand, was the epitome of a lazy stoner. Not that she had anything against pot. She'd smoked it a handful of times, usually when she was too drunk to really realize what she was doing.

"So what route you taking?" said Chad.

"I was going to try 21," said Max. "It's a smaller highway, and there aren't any tolls or anything... so I don't think anyone would think to block that."

"Sounds good," said Mandy. "I could see that working. And then we'll head west for a while until we head north?"

"Yup," said Max.

"I don't know," said Chad. "Do you remember when we were kids, Max, and we had that mini tornado?"

"Mini tornado?" said Mandy. "What's that? Is that even a real thing, or some pothead day dream?"

Chad ignored her.

"It was real," said Max. "Some kind of freak storm. What about it, Chad?"

"Well," said Chad. "When that happened, everyone was freaking out and we all got stuck on 21, remember?"

"Where were you going? Why were you leaving the area?"

"The power was out for like two weeks," said Max. "Everyone wanted to go stay in hotels."

"That's not going to be happening now," said Chad. "No hotels are going to have power either... Shit, I wonder if this is all over the country or just here in PA, or just on the Eastern seaboard or what."

Mandy crossed her arms in annoyance. She didn't understand how this fat stoner was so easily grasping exactly what was happening. It had taken her much longer to grasp the seriousness of the problem, and she felt silly and stupid now. Plus, Max had this rapport already with Chad, whereas she'd just met Max. So far, she was impressed with him. The fact that he saved her life probably had something to do with that. Frankly, she was a little jealous of Chad.

"We'll avoid 21 then," said Max. "Good point, Chad. Even if people aren't going to hotels, they'll be trying to leave... for somewhere. But my suspicions are that this is something that happened all over the country, not just here."

"How do you know?" said Mandy.

"There's no way to know," said Max. "Not without communication."

"Maybe we could get some smoke signals going once we make camp," said Chad, chuckling at his own joke.

"I bet you're an expert at that," said Mandy.

"I'll just keep driving west on these back roads," said Max. "Mandy and Chad, you guys check the atlas there and the maps that you brought. It's a good thing you had those. See if you can find a good route. I know my way around here, but there might be something better..."

They drove on through the night in silence.

There weren't many cars on the road now.

Mandy realized that it was *very* good that Max had extra gasoline in the back of the Jeep. She could smell it, and the smell made her a little sick, but if this EMP was a reality, then she doubted the gas pumps would work.

Mandy figured that people had realized that this wasn't just a blackout. This was something more. The mob back at Chad's store proved that.

But what she was confused about was why there weren't more cars on the road. It was eerie, especially considering how black the night was. She had never seen darkness like this. The headlights from the Jeep barely seemed to cut through it. They just drilled little holes of light into the night in front of them, holes that disappeared a moment later, swallowed by the darkness.

Maybe if people realized it wasn't a blackout, they would also realize that they didn't have much gas left. Maybe they weren't driving around because they wanted to save their gasoline. Another factor was that they were no longer driving on the main roads at all. And it was the middle of the night... Still, something was strange about it. Maybe people were barricading themselves in their houses... Maybe they were terrified to leave...

Mandy wondered what she would be doing right now if Max hadn't come along. Well, she'd have been raped and possibly killed. But if that hadn't happened, she couldn't see herself venturing out of the apartment building, let alone her own apartment. Maybe that was why people weren't on the road—fear, pure and simple.

But what about that mob?

Mandy shuddered as she thought about the animalistic anger she'd seen on that man's face as he rushed towards the Jeep.

"You guys mind if I light up?" said Chad.

Mandy could hear him pulling something out of his cargo pocket.

"Yes," said Max simply.

"You sure?" said Chad. "I've got enough for all three of us. Could help us relax, you know?"

"Are you crazy?" said Mandy.

"I'm not crazy, just trying to relax."

"I take back what I said about being sorry," said Mandy. "You really are going to be a liability. Are you just going to be interested in getting high while the world ends?"

"Mandy," said Max, trying to calm her down.

"What?" she snarled at him. "I'm not allowed to speak my mind?"

Suddenly, the Jeep ran over something. There was a thud that didn't sound good as the Jeep bounced on its suspension.

"What was that?"

"Shit."

Max didn't say anything.

He slowed the Jeep to a stop.

"I think we blew a tire," he said. He put the Jeep into neutral and engaged the emergency brake.

Mandy noticed that he didn't kill the engine. And he didn't get out of the car yet. Instead, he killed the headlights and studied the darkness that surrounded them.

"You think someone's out there?" whispered Mandy.

"Can you see what it was we ran over?" said Max in a low voice.

"No," she said.

"I can't see anything either," said Chad.

Max and Mandy both ignored him.

"You think this is a trap or something?" said Mandy. Her heart was pounding in her chest as she peered into the darkness around them. She couldn't see anything, but that didn't mean anything.

"I don't know," said Max. "Could be. Might not be. I don't know what we ran over."

"Don't get out of the car," whispered Mandy.

"I have to," said Max. "Someone's got to change this tire."

The car was noticeably sagging on Mandy's side.

Max flicked on his flashlight, on the lowest setting. Mandy saw him reaching for his gun. He had it in his hand now.

"What do we do?" said Chad.

"Stay in the car," said Max. "And don't you dare light that joint. I need you as lucid as you're going to get."

Mandy's heart felt like it was beating so fast that it would burst right through her chest.

She watched with terrible anxiety as Max slowly opened his door.

"I don't want to hurt anyone," said Mr. McKinney.

"I don't want anyone to get hurt either," said Georgia.

"Then put your gun down."

Georgia knew she had no other choice. She couldn't risk James getting killed. If he was shot in the stomach, that might be the end. He'd bleed out... Who knew if the hospitals were even open. This was a panic situation, the type of situation in which normal people did things they never would do otherwise. For all she knew, Mr. McKinney could pull the trigger by accident. After all, his finger was inside the trigger guard. He looked jumpy and nervous. In the dim light of the camping lantern, she could see that his eye was twitching.

Georgia slowly put the rifle to the ground. "I'm lowering it to the ground," she said, speaking slowly and as calmly as she could.

Her thoughts turned to Sadie in the car, and she hoped that she was OK. She also hoped she'd stay in the car, rather than come looking for them.

"Good," grunted Mr. McKinney. "Good."

Georgia laid the rifle on the ground and stood back up slowly.

"Look," she said. "I get it, you're angry. We were coming to steal your supplies, that's true."

"So you admit it then." He still had his gun trained on James's stomach, and he didn't show any signs of pointing it somewhere else.

"I admit it," said Georgia. "But I thought you weren't here, and that you weren't coming back. A cop just told us that the whole area was blocked off. We figured no one else had been able to get home from work."

"Well I'm here, aren't I?"

"Look, we've known each other a long time. Do you think I'd actually try to hurt your family?"

"I heard you say it yourself. You said it was either your family or mine. Well, I'm going to have to make the same decision."

"Please, don't hurt James. If you need to shoot someone, shoot me instead. But shooting us isn't going to help anything."

"No!" said James. "Mom, don't say that."

"Don't say another word," said Mr. McKinney, glaring at James. His finger on the trigger seemed to be shaking.

"Look, Mark," said Georgia. "This is a crazy situation... Let's just forget this ever happened, OK? We're going to go back to our truck and drive away..."

"What if you come back?" said Mr. McKinney. "I've got to think about my family."

Georgia suddenly realized that the rest of the McKinneys must be inside.

Suddenly, a voice spoke from the dark.

Georgia recognized it instantly. It was Sadie.

"Drop the gun," said Sadie, speaking from the darkness. "I've got a rifle pointed right at your head, and my mom's been taking me to shooting practice since I was eight."

Sadie was bluffing. Georgia just hoped that Mark McKinney didn't know that. But he was at work most of the time. He probably hadn't noticed whether or not Sadie was heading off to the shooting range with Georgia or not.

"I don't believe you," said Mr. McKinney.

Georgia prayed silently that Sadie actually had a gun with her. If she was still scared of even touching guns, she wouldn't have brought the gun with her. Then there was no chance. Georgia was seriously regretting her plan to rob her neighbors.

Sadie stepped out of the shadows. She was across from Georgia, at a right angle from where Mr. McKinney was pointing his gun.

Sadie held one of Georgia's hunting rifles. She held it like she knew what she was doing. Her finger was inside the trigger guard, on the trigger.

Georgia looked at the gun, realized which one it was, and knew that it wasn't loaded.

Georgia prayed silently to herself, to no one, to anything at all, that Sadie could pull this off. Mark McKinney seemed to be getting less stable by the minute. The more worried and the more anxious he got, the more likely he was to do something rash, and his gun was still pointed at James's stomach.

"Drop the gun, Mark," said Georgia.

"Drop it," said Sadie.

Georgia was impressed. Sadie was holding the gun like a pro, and speaking like a pro. It must have been all the

gunslinger movies she'd watched with Georgia when
growing up. There were always standoffs in those movies,
and the guy who won was usually the guy with the coolest
demeanor, the guy who was the most relaxed and the most
sure of himself and his abilities.

Sadie held the gun.

"OK," said Mark McKinney. "I'm dropping it. But I want
you off my property."

"Whatever you want," said Georgia.

He dropped the gun to the ground.

Georgia moved towards him and scooped it up. She put
it in in the waistband of her jeans. It might be useful later.
She had no intention of giving it back to him, not to the man
who'd pointed a gun at her son's stomach.

"Good work, Sadie," said Georgia. "Now give me
the gun."

"Thank God," said Sadie, handing the gun to Georgia.
Sadie was visibly shaken as she handed the gun over. Her
cool demeanor had vanished. You could see she didn't like
even touching the gun. "I don't have any idea how to
use it."

"You did great," said Georgia, knowing not to mention
that it wasn't loaded.

"A trick!" shouted Mark McKinney.

"Stay where you are," said Georgia, pointing the rifle
at him.

He looked her right in the eyes and he looked
completely terrified.

"Where's your family?" said Georgia. "Are they inside?"

Mark nodded.

"No one's going to ask if I'm OK?" said James. "That nut
job was going to shoot me."

"Grow up, James," said Georgia. "You're fine. Now go into

the shed and check for gas. We're going to need extra gas if we're going to make it up to the hunting cabin."

"You're going to rob me anyway!"

"We'll leave your food and water," said Georgia. She realized she might regret this decision later. But she couldn't leave them here to die...

James was back a couple minutes later, holding his flashlight in his mouth. He had two cans of gas meant for a lawnmower, one in each hand.

"Let's go," she said to her kids. "And don't move, Mark. I'm taking the gun. I don't think you have the balls to shoot someone anyway."

James loaded the gas cans, they all got in, and Georgia backed out of the driveway.

"Well that went well," said Sadie sarcastically. "Looks like James should have done a better job being a perv and spying on Mrs. McKinney."

"Shut up," said James. "I'm the one who almost died."

"He wasn't going to shoot anyone," said Georgia, but she wasn't so sure she was speaking the truth.

Georgia drove slowly down the darkened street. The pitch black night seemed to swallow them up. The absence of light pollution was creepy. Not a single star shone in the sky. It was cloudy. The moon was gone, completely invisible.

"Mom," said James. "I don't get it. How are we going to get out of here? You heard the cop, the road is blocked off."

Georgia didn't say anything for a moment. "We're just going to have to find another way."

She was racking her brains for ideas. She couldn't think of anything. How could they get out, if not for roads?

Then, an idea occurred to her.

It would be dangerous. It would be risky. It would be kind of crazy.

But there was a slight chance it might work.

And that just might save their lives.

Crazy ideas were just the kind of ideas she was looking for right now. The normal things wouldn't work. Nothing was normal now, and it might never be again.

"**D**on't go out there, Max," said Mandy from the passenger seat.

"Yeah, man," said Chad from the backseat. "I've got a bad feeling about this."

"What other choice do we have?" said Max.

He had his hand on the door handle. He had a bad feeling about getting out of the Jeep.

But Max didn't believe in permission. He believed in thinking rationally, logically. Not that he always managed it all the time. But who could?

"I'll come with you," said Mandy.

"Shit, then I'm coming too," said Chad.

Max didn't need to think about it much.

"Mandy, you come with me. Take the flashlight from the glove box. Chad, you stay here."

"Aw, man," said Chad.

"You're too high to be useful," said Max. Even though Chad was an old friend, Max didn't have any problem speaking to him directly, even if it was harsh. This wasn't the time to consider how people felt about things.

Max opened the door to the Jeep and got out. He left it running in case they had to make a quick escape. Not that they could get far on a busted tire.

"Maybe we should drive farther down," whispered Mandy, appearing next to him in the darkness.

They both turned their flashlights on. They were high power LED flashlights, but the brighter they were set to, the faster the battery would die. And there was no way to recharge them now. Max needed to conserve the batteries. He had his on the second to lowest setting, and showed Mandy how to do the same.

"Maybe you're right," muttered Max. "But the farther we go, the greater the risk of damaging the wheel."

He and Mandy shone their lights around the area.

"You see anything?" said Mandy

"Nope," said Max. "I think we're OK."

He had to dig around in the back for a while to get out the jack and the wrench. There was so much gear covering everything that it took a little while. Fortunately, the spare tire was easily accessible on the back of the car.

Max hated to change a tire out so early. They had many miles to go, and that was the only spare tire. Yet another chink in his armor, yet another problem with his plans, yet another thing that he hadn't planned like he should have. He'd thought he was prepared. Maybe he was doing better than some others, but it wasn't good enough. He did have some of that chemical aerosol goop that you could spray into a tire, but Max didn't like the idea of that. And it might be possible in the future to patch the tire, but Max only know how that would work in theory. He'd never actually done it before.

At some point, Max realized it might be good to turn the car off. There didn't seem to be anyone there, anyway. And with a wheel off, it wasn't like having the engine on would help them get away any faster. So he killed the engine.

"How's it going out there?" said Chad.

"Shut up, Chad," said Max.

Chad shut up, and Max got out of the car again and started to work. He loosened the bolts, got the jack set up, and then got the spare tire on.

Mandy stood guard, surveying the area carefully with her flashlight's long beam. Anyway, for now, it was good that she kept the light turned on. Max was still a little worried that there might be someone out there.

While Max worked, his thoughts turned to Chad. How strange was it that he'd run into Chad there, in a situation like that? He hadn't seen Chad in how many years? He couldn't even remember in this moment. But his mind felt frazzled. He'd been awake for a long time, and his body was starting to crave sleep. But there were many hours and miles to go. He didn't totally trust Mandy behind the wheel, given the unknowns in the situation. And he definitely didn't trust Chad.

He'd felt an obligation to rescue Chad, but he knew he couldn't count on him. Chad had let him down countless times in the past. Not only that, but Chad had let everyone down. They'd tried to have an intervention for him, but it was hopeless. It had been terrible, and Max shuddered at the memory now. He wondered if Chad even remembered it.

"Everything fine?" said Max, to Mandy.

"Fine," she said, speaking in a low but audible voice.

The car door opened and Chad got out. His weight shifted the car and Max could feel it.

"Surprised you could lift the car up with me in it," joked Chad.

"I'm almost done," grunted Max, as he started lowering the car.

Next, he set to work tightening the bolts, working in a star pattern as he'd been taught.

"I think we're all set," said Max. "I almost want to say we should investigate what we ran over, but maybe it'd be better not to."

"Yeah," said Mandy. "Let's just keep going. This place gives me the creeps."

It *was* creepy. Max didn't want to admit it to himself. But there was something a little strange about this area.

There weren't any houses around. Either side of the road was just woods, possibly stretching for miles. They'd already left the suburbs without quite realizing it. The suburbs had just sort of gradually faded away, and without light on in the houses, it was hard to tell how densely populated the area was that they'd left.

"Well," said Max. "I guess we're doing good. We're away from most of the chaos. The less densely populated the area we're in, the better."

The sound of lighter came through the night. Chad was sparking up a joint.

"Chad!" hissed Max. "What the hell are you doing?"

"Just relaxing, man," said Chad, speaking in a strange voice as he held the smoke deep in his lungs.

He exhaled and started coughing. It was a loud cough that seemed to echo all round them in the silent night.

Max suddenly realized there wasn't a single other sound. It was dead quiet.

Mandy realized it at the same time, too. "There aren't even any animals here," she said, as she stared off into the depths of the dark woods.

"Let's get going," said Max. "Chad, put that out, OK?"

"OK, man," said Chad, licking his fingers to extinguish the joint and presumably save it for later.

The whole area now reeked of weed, and Max had always hated the smell. It reminded him of something wet and rotting.

Max was halfway into the driver's seat when Chad, who was still standing around fiddling with his joint, shouted.

"What is it?" said Mandy, worried.

She was already in the passenger's seat, and she shut the door quickly.

"Shit, man, did you see that?" said Chad.

"What was it?" said Max.

"I don't know, man... Eyes... A pair of eyes off in the woods there..."

"Get in the car," said Max.

Chad got in, and his weight shifted the suspension of the Jeep.

"Let's hope this tire holds up," said Max, hitting the button to lock all the doors. He considered putting the child safety lock on, in case Chad tried something, but he thought better of it.

"What did you see?" said Mandy, turning around to face him in the darkness.

"Eyes," said Chad. His tone was hushed. He sounded really worried. "But they weren't normal eyes."

"What do you mean?"

"I mean, they were definitely human... But there was something..."

"Come on," said Max. "This isn't a zombie movie."

"I know," said Chad. "But it was something... Maybe it was someone watching us."

"You're just high," said Max. "You're paranoid."

"Maybe," muttered Chad. "Maybe..."

"I'm worried about it," said Mandy.

"Don't be," said Max.

The three of them didn't talk much for the next few hours. Despite Max's growing fatigue, he continued to drive. He kept his speed at about forty miles an hour, which seemed reasonable on these roads. He didn't want to go too slow, or too fast. Too slow and they'd never get there. Too fast, and he'd just waste fuel and increase the chances of either an accident or something else. He couldn't afford to blow another tire. Not now.

He tried not to accelerate much, and not to brake much either. Both actions would merely waste fuel. He shifted frequently to conserve more fuel, and when he could, he put the Jeep in neutral and let it coast down the long hills.

Chad eventually started snoring, falling fast asleep into his drug filled dreams.

Mandy stayed awake, although she was starting to fade a little.

Max was starting to become glad that he'd brought her along. It turned out that she was really good with maps, and figuring out where they were. Max didn't want to admit it to himself, but reading maps had never been his strong suit. Sure, he could study a map and understand it, but when it came to figuring out where his actual location was... well, that just wasn't his strong suit.

"Take a left here," said Mandy.

They'd come to a fork in the road, and Max sat with the engine idling.

"You sure?" he said. "It seems like that way takes us east."

"I'm positive," said Mandy.

Max was surprised that he already trusted her so much. He took the left, accelerating slowly into the curve.

"You tired?" said Max.

"Yeah," said Mandy, sleepily.

"Me too," said Max. "But I figure the farther away we get, the better. Then we'll have to shift strategies. In the future, it'll be safer to keep ourselves well rested and well fed. But I think I'm OK for now."

"This is a stupid question," said Mandy. "But do you have any coffee or anything?"

Max gestured to the thermos that he normally took to work. Mandy took it from the cup holder and greedily gulped down the small amount that remained.

"That's not going to be enough," she said.

"I didn't think of it before," said Max. "But I might have some caffeine pills in the glove compartment."

"Why didn't you tell me?" said Mandy, fishing around frantically in the glove compartment.

She found the bottle, shook out two pills without reading the label, and swallowed them dry.

"Here," she said. "You're getting too sleepy to drive."

"Give me three," said Max.

He took them from her carefully with his eyes still on the road. He wasn't good at swallowing pills dry, and had to take them one at a time.

Max started feel much more alert within just a few minutes. That made sense, since he didn't have any food in his stomach, and they weren't slow release pills.

"I should have thought of that before," said Max.

"It's OK," said Mandy.

"It's not," said Max. "You know, I thought I was all organized and prepared, but... I don't even know where half my gear is. It's buried somewhere in the back of the Jeep with Chad."

"You're doing great," said Mandy softly. "I shudder to

think where I'd be without you... And you saved your friend from that mob."

"I don't know if he's exactly a friend," said Max quietly. "I mean, we were friends... really close. Like I said, or maybe I thought it—I can't remember now. I've been up for too long. I'm starting to ramble. Anyway, he's more like family. A family member you just can't get rid of, but one you have to try to help."

Mandy didn't say anything for a while.

The night was still pitch black. The clouds covered the stars and possibly the moon, depending on what phase of the cycle it was. Max had no idea, but he supposed it wasn't anything close to a full moon, since that tended to illuminate things through the clouds.

Max felt better with the caffeine, and he felt better getting out of the densely populated suburban areas. He congratulated himself again for not taking a job in the city. Who knew what kind of hellish fate awaited the people stuck in the cities. Maybe they'd already turned into one huge angry chaotic mob, fighting each other to the death. And in a week or two? They might be eating each other. It wasn't a joke. Max had read about the Donner party, and that rugby team that had crashed landed. Sooner or later, when humans ran out of food, they started eating each other. Usually they had the decency to wait until they were dead, but not always. Sometimes necessity dictated that someone be killed, or a lot of people be killed.

The road was in good condition. Max was able to easily swerve around the occasional pothole. The trees were thick and tall, creating a blanket of intense darkness on either side of them. The road was straight in parts for long stretches, with an occasional section of dense curves. At another time, Max would relish this type of driving. He still loved the feeling of shifting gears in the Jeep, his foot on the clutch applying just the right amount of force. He loved the feeling of the engine connected directly to the wheels as he downshifted into a curve.

"Does he just smoke pot?" said Mandy, breaking the silence.

"Huh?" said Max.

Chad snored on in the backseat.

"I mean does he do other drugs?"

"I don't know. Why?"

"If he does harder stuff, he might go into withdrawal... I've seen it before at work. One of the girls was sniffing coke in the bathroom. Then once on one shift, the manager had some stomach problems and was in the bathroom the whole time. It was busy, and she couldn't sneak off anywhere else. By the end of the shift, she was going nuts, screaming at customers and everything. I guess she was addicted pretty badly..."

"Where did you work?" said Max.

"It was at some Thai restaurant," said Mandy.

"Well," said Max. "I don't know, honestly. I haven't talked to him in years. In the past, it was mostly pot and alcohol, with the occasional pill. I think he was pretty into ecstasy for a while."

"Oh, well that's not addictive."

"You sound like you know from personal experience."

"Maybe," said Mandy. "That's all in my past now. I mean... yeah... in my past."

"Good," said Max, simply. The truth was, her past didn't matter to him now. Most of the past didn't matter. This was a new start. Everything would be new. The future was what mattered now, if there was a future to be had, that is.

"Anyway," said Mandy. "Even if he's just a really heavy drinker, he's going to go into withdrawal."

Max shrugged, even though Mandy couldn't see his gesture in the darkness. "He'll just have to deal with it," said Max.

"It might not be that easy."

They continued to drive in silence. Mandy turned her flashlight on, and Max had to tell her to put it on the lowest setting. It was just one candlepower, but it was enough that she could study the map. She was poring over it, really trying to understand it.

"Now we have a choice coming up," said Mandy. "There's a town about ten miles up ahead. A small town. Population 1,200, if the back of the atlas is right."

"Probably about right," said Max.

"We can go through the town," said Mandy. "Or we can go around it."

"Around it," said Max.

"Yeah, that's what I thought too. I mean, like you're always saying... the less populated an area, the safer we'll be, right?"

"Yup," said Max. "We're going around it."

"OK, but here's the thing," said Mandy. "If we go around it, we're adding at least three hours to our trip."

"Three hours? Are you sure."

"Something like that," said Mandy. "Maybe more, actually."

"Damnit," said Max. "We can't afford to lose that much fuel."

"I thought you had the extra gas in the back."

"I do, but that's just about enough to get us there. We can't count on the gas stations working."

"That's what I figured, but I thought you had enough."

"I do... But we've got all this gear. We've got two more people than I'd counted on. And that takes up gas. And Chad counts as two. If we have to take another detour later on... No, we can't do it. We're going through the town."

"But what about that mob we rescued Chad from?"

"We?" said Max.

Mandy didn't answer.

"I thought it sounded like you were trying to convince me to go around the town."

"I don't know what to do," said Mandy. "You make the decision. It's your car."

"We're going through it," said Max. "Maybe everyone will be asleep."

"It's probably just a couple buildings off of the road anyway," said Mandy. "I bet we'll just drive right through it."

"What's this town named anyway?" said Max.

"Marxburg," said Mandy.

"Never heard of it," said Max.

They drove on. The ten miles went quickly. They only had the sound of Chad's intense snoring to keep them company.

Max rolled his window down partially and let the cool air flow over him. It felt good and kept him awake. He wasn't exactly anxious, but perhaps a little preoccupied with what might happen in the town.

They'd climbed up one of those short Pennsylvania "mountains" which in other areas of the country would be considered nothing more than large hills.

They were on the descent when they spotted the town. Max had the car in neutral, and they were gaining momentum on the straight downward stretch of road. He put the car into fourth to engine brake, and then third, and then second. He didn't want to be going too fast through the town.

"Shit," said Max.

"What's happening?" said Chad, suddenly waking up and sounding startled.

"They've got something in the road," said Mandy.

Indeed they did. There was something in the road all right, but Max didn't have any idea what it was. From this distance, it just looked like a pile of crap stacked up in the road.

"What the hell?" said Max.

He applied the brakes and slowed the Jeep down even more.

As they got closer, they could see more clearly what was in front of them. It really was a huge pile of junk that had been piled in the middle of the road. It looked like a rudimentary road block, or a shield behind which soldiers would hide in battle. It was made of old couches, chairs, dining room tables, cardboard boxes, all manner of things.

"Can we go through it?" said Mandy.

Max stopped the car about a hundred meters in front of the big pile of junk.

"Just blast through it, man," said Chad, who immediately started coughing intensely after he spoke.

"I don't think we can go through it," said Max. He studied the pile carefully. It turned out that it wasn't just made of furniture. There were some steel rods that ran through the structure. Max couldn't tell how it was constructed, but he figured the thing had a steel skeleton. "Whoever made this didn't want cars to go through it. If we try, I think they'll already have some kind of plan in place for that."

"Then what do we do?"

"Don't move a muscle, or I won't hesitate to put one right through your skull," came a stranger's voice from outside the car.

Max moved only his eyes. In his peripheral vision, he could just barely make out a man standing next to the driver's side door.

Slowly, the man moved closer. He moved his gun until the cold metal muzzle was pressed again the side of Max's head.

Max didn't dare even open his mouth to speak.

"Mom, we can't go over that."

"Do you know another way out of here, James?" said Georgia.

She had the pickup stopped right in front of the old covered bridge that ran across the local river. The river didn't have a name as far as Georgia knew. It wasn't that big. But it had been once, and while the water level may have only been a trickle, long, long ago the rushing and flowing waters had eroded a sizable canyon. It was known in the neighborhood as the moat, because it essentially cut off all access to the neighborhood.

The only other way out was blocked by the police.

This covered bridge hadn't been used in at least fifteen years. But there it stood, made of wood, incredibly small, impossibly rickety looking. It looked like it might fall at the slightest breeze.

The township had been talking about putting up a new bridge, or at least tearing this one down, ever since the bridge had been declared off limits. A sign had been put up along with a stupid little gate that blocked unknowing cars from trying to cross it. The engineers had long ago deemed the bridge completely unsafe. It should have been replaced a long time ago, but no one could agree on the new bridge or how much money to spend on it. The result was that there it still stood.

"We're going to die, aren't we?" said Sadie, sounding worried.

"I don't know what else to do, kids," said Georgia. "If we stay there, well, you saw how crazy Mark McKinney had gotten..."

"To be fair, you were trying to steal all his food."

"Don't act like it was just me," said Georgia. "Plus, we had our reasons."

"Well," said Georgia. "Here goes nothing."

She knew she was putting the lives of her and her children at risk. But it was more of a risk to stay put in the neighborhood.

She pushed her foot down on the accelerator. The last thought she had, as they started to race towards the out-of-commission bridge, was that she should have first driven by to see if the police barricade really had been up. But she'd had her reasons not to do that—what if the police themselves became violent, or what if there was a mob of people there, ready to commit violent acts against her family.

The pickup slammed right through the flimsy metal gate, knocking it down.

"Here we go!" shouted James. He sounded more excited than worried.

Georgia felt a thrill run through her as they made it halfway across the bridge.

"We're going to die!" shouted Sadie. "Shit, shit, shit."

Georgia didn't say anything. She just kept her foot

pressed firmly on the accelerator. The engine roared. The tachometer was at the red line.

The bridge creaked audibly beneath them. The wood was shifting. Some part of the wooden structure was twisting. She could feel it beneath the truck.

But they made it across.

Georgia let out a whoop when the truck rushed onto solid land.

"Don't look back," she said.

But Sadie did anyway.

"It's completely twisted!"

The truck was moving too fast. Georgia had to turn the wheel sharply to avoid running into a tree. They narrowly missed it.

"Mom!" shouted Sadie.

"It's fine," said Georgia, as she regained control of the sliding and speeding truck.

They were now barreling down Solomon Street. It was tree lined, and there were plenty of houses.

"Damn, look at those," said James, in awe of the enormous houses.

"That's where Josh lives," said Sadie, pointing to one.

The lights were all off, and the buildings could only be seen by the faint diffuse glow coming off the penetrating high beams of the truck.

"I guess the generators aren't working," said Georgia. "Or maybe they don't have any."

They didn't pass any cars as they continued west.

"It won't take us that long to get there," said Georgia. "If we drive all night, I bet we can be there by morning. If we don't run into any trouble, that is."

"So do you think they'll be like bandits out?" said James.

"You know, roving bands of guys, like in the movies. Armed to the teeth and all that?"

"Shut up, James," said Sadie. "You're an idiot."

"What?" said James. "I know what I'm talking about. I've studied up."

"I wouldn't exactly call watching a bunch of violent movies studying up on what happens when the power goes out."

"It's not just the power, idiot, remember?"

"Kids!" shouted Georgia. "Quiet! No more arguing, OK?"

They agreed demurely.

"And I don't think we'll be running into any armed bandits," said Georgia. "The situation may be dire, but in those movies that takes quite a while to happen, right, James?"

"I guess so," said James.

"They're just movies!" said Sadie, frustrated. "They're not real. Both of you need to calm down."

"Well, Sadie, your brother does have a point. You saw how Mr. McKinney was acting..."

Neither one responded. They were probably tired of Georgia's constant refrain at this point.

Georgia continued to drive through the night. Sadie fell asleep and James's snores eventually came up to the front of the cabin of the truck.

Georgia felt wired and awake. She'd occasionally worked late shifts and night shifts, and she knew how to keep herself alert. She didn't need coffee or caffeine, she just needed to have her mind fixed on something, on a goal. Right now, her goal was getting herself and her kids to safety. The farther they were from whatever it was that was going on, the better.

Georgia picked up Sadie's smartphone from the cup

holder. She held it idly in her hand as she drove and wondered if it would ever work again. It wasn't the smartphone itself that was important, but what it represented.

Georgia wondered if this was happening all over the world. If global communications were done completely, it could send the world back to the dark ages.

Yeah, she thought, the farther away the better.

Georgia knew the route well, and she hoped they'd be there by morning. She didn't need maps or a GPS device. She drove intuitively, as she'd already done many times before in her life.

She still had the pistol she'd taken from the McKinneys tucked in her waistband. Of course, she'd made sure the safety was on. Now that it was there, it felt like a comforting weight. She liked the feel of it there. She wondered how she'd gone this long without getting a concealed carry license.

Georgia kept her eye on the gas gauge. Unfortunately, it had been a little while since she'd filled up the tank. The gauge registered half full. That *might* be enough to make it there, considering that she could coast down some of the hills to save gas. But sometimes the gauge on this old truck could be inaccurate, registering the tank fuller than it actually was.

It was a good thing she'd taken that gas from the McKinneys.

They'd driven for hours now. It was 4 o'clock in the morning, and the area was deserted. They were out towards central Pennsylvania, where the houses and towns were scarcer than in the suburbs. The ones they'd passed had been completely dark, with no one out. They hadn't passed a single car yet on the roads. That wasn't that unusual though, considering they were on back roads, the less-traveled ones, the ones that Georgia had always preferred. If it hadn't been for her kids needing to go to a good school system, Georgia imagined she might have liked to live out west somewhere, where there weren't so many people, where you could be more free.

When she was sure there was nothing around them but the forest, Georgia slowed to a stop, pulling off to the side of the road.

"What's going on, Mom?" said James from the back, waking up.

"I'm trying to sleep!" said Sadie, waking up briefly and speaking sleepily before settling back down to sleep. Sadie had always been a good sleeper. Sure, things could wake her up, but she always went right back to her dreams.

"I need your help, James," said Georgia.

"What's going on?"

"There's no need to keep waking up your sister. Get out of the car and I'll explain it to you."

They both got out of the truck, which was turned off.

"We might be running low on gas," said Georgia.

"You didn't fill it up?"

"I didn't exactly have a chance," said Georgia.

"Sorry," said James.

"I'm going to pour in the gas that you got from the McKinneys' shed. That way we won't run out when we aren't expecting it. I don't really trust the gas gauge on this old truck any more. And I'll feel better knowing we have plenty of gas."

"What do you want me to do?"

"You watch," said Georgia. "Keep a lookout."

She reached into the bed of the truck and took a loaded rifle. She handed it to James. She was glad that at least one of her kids actually knew how to use a gun.

"Got it," said James.

The night was black, and despite the light from her flashlight, Georgia could barely see James's face. If she could have, she would have liked to imagine that James wore an expression of grim determination. Good, she thought, it was time her kids grew up. Sadie was already getting there—she never would have guessed that she could have pulled off that stunt with the gun back at the McKinneys. She had a ways to go, sure, but she'd get there. The situation would force them all to evolve, to change, to do what was necessary in order to survive.

With her flashlight, Georgia got the plastic jugs of gas out and set them down on the pavement. She removed the gas cap from the truck. Next, she found a funnel that had been lying in the bed of the truck for as long as she could remember. She didn't remember why she had it but she was glad she did.

She had some brief worry as she tipped the gas jug up, letting it flow into the truck, but a second later it was gone from her mind. She couldn't remember what it was. Maybe she was more tired than she'd thought.

"OK," she said. "I got it. It's all in there."

She tightened the gas cap back on, and slapped the truck's side for good measure.

She and James clamored back into the truck.

"Let's hope that's enough to get us there," she said, as she cranked the engine.

Immediately upon turning the key, she knew something was wrong.

The engine started making a horribly loud churning noise.

"Turn it off!" shouted James.

"What's going on?" said Sadie, waking up again.

Georgia kept the engine on. And it kept making the horrible sound. The truck was shaking.

"What's happening?" said James.

The smell was horrible, like burned oil mixed with something else.

"The gas must have been for the lawnmower."

"So what? It's still gas."

"Some lawnmowers take oil right in the tank..." She couldn't believe James didn't know that. Hadn't she taught him anything?

"What's going to happen?" said Sadie. She sounded scared.

"Maybe it'll be OK," said Georgia, as she continued to listen to the horrible sounds the truck was making. But she knew intuitively that it wouldn't be OK. She had poured a lot of gas into the engine. "Normally I'd turn it off and drain the tank, to save the engine. But it looks like we don't have any choice but to try to drive it and see what happens. It doesn't have to work after we get there... we just have to get there."

She put the truck in gear and pressed the accelerator gingerly.

The truck made an even worse series of sounds.

It lurched forward a few feet, as if its driver was someone who was just learning how to drive a stick shift car.

"Shit," muttered Georgia, as the truck lurched to a complete and sudden stop. No matter how much she pressed the accelerator, nothing happened. It made one last loud noise and Georgia cut the engine. She didn't think it would cause a fire, but she couldn't risk it, considering that all their possessions were in the truck.

Georgia got out of the cab to open the hood. Oily black smoke billowed up at her. She started coughing.

"Mom!" said James, putting his arms around her and pulling her away from the engine.

"Shit," said Georgia, again.

There were tears in her eyes, and she wasn't the type of woman who cried. But she was so worried about James and Sadie. The three of them needed to get to the hunting cabin. Once people started really freaking out, they'd be trying to get out to this area, to the less inhabited places, where there were animals you could hunt and places you could grow food. And a lot of those people would become ruthless and cutthroat. Georgia shuddered to think what might happen to James, and Sadie... especially Sadie. Sadie was at the age where Georgia had to argue with her to make her put on less revealing clothing. Men were always checking her out when they were out in public. Georgia usually just said something scathing to the men, who turned red from embarrassment. But if society collapsed, the rules would be different.

But if they were in the hunting cabin, they'd be far removed from everything. It was an area that was difficult to access without a truck. On foot? It would take forever. Georgia could defend her family from there. But it also meant that there wasn't much of a chance of them getting there without a truck or an SUV.

Georgia was feeling anxious. She didn't normally feel anxious. It felt like she couldn't breathe. It felt like the world was crashing down around her.

She sat down on the side of the road, on a rock. She put her head in her hands and wished that everything would go away. She wished it was yesterday. She wished that this had never happened.

"It's going to be OK, Mom," said Sadie, sitting down next to Georgia and putting her arm around her.

"We'll figure a way out of this," said James, sitting down on the other side of her.

But Georgia knew it wouldn't be OK. They had all their gear in the truck. They wouldn't survive without it. But she had no way of carrying it without the truck. She didn't have backpacks designed to carry a lot of gear. And there was no way they could hike that far anyway... Well, maybe...

But Georgia knew that they needed another vehicle, one that could traverse the tough terrain on the way to the hunting cabin.

And the only way to get another vehicle?

Steal one.

12

"**W**ho are you with?" said the stranger's voice.

Max didn't dare to even move his mouth to speak. He didn't need to give this guy an excuse to shoot him.

If only they'd taken the long way around that town... But it was too late now.

Max hoped that Mandy and especially Chad would have enough sense not to speak.

"Who are you with?" screamed the man. "Answer me!"

"It's just us," said Max, not really understanding the question.

His eyes were fixed ahead towards the strange barrier on the entrance to the town. Behind it, on either side of the road, he could see two squat buildings. One looked like It was some kind of general store, and the other might have been a bar.

Despite the intensity of the situation, Max's mind was again on practical matters: he was burning a lot of fuel just sitting here idly. He knew he had to ask if it was OK to kill the engine. If they got out of this situation, they needed to have all the gas they could.

"Who sent you?" shouted the man. He sounded angry and confused. "The Chinese? The Russians?"

"No," said Max, trying to keep his voice as calm and steady as he could. He didn't need to give this guy with the gun more of a reason to get upset. "We're not working with any foreign governments."

"Then why are you here?"

Max hesitated for a moment. He didn't quite know how to put it. "The power was out in our area. Everyone was going crazy. We're just trying to get out... We're just like you... just looking for a way to survive."

"Bullshit," shouted the man. "This is some kind of attack. Nothing works! The TV's out. The radio!"

"It's the same in our area," said Max.

"Shut the hell up!" shouted the man, pressing the muzzle of the gun further into Max's head.

"Look, man," said Chad. "We're not trying to do you guys no harm or nothing..."

"Shut up!" shouted the man. "Everyone, out of the trees!" It sounded like he was shouting a command to a group of people.

Sure enough, a moment later, people started emerging from the trees. Max could hear their footsteps approaching, but he didn't want to turn his head, not with the gun against him.

Max didn't know how many people there were.

They opened the doors of the Jeep, reaching through the windows to unlock them. Hands dragged Max out of the driver's seat.

Something smashed into Max's head and he fell unconscious.

The next thing he knew, he woke up in some back room somewhere. There was the new light of morning streaming through the windows. He felt dizzy and nauseous and his head ached terribly.

His whole body was stiff with pain and he felt like he could barely move. He wasn't yet totally aware of everything. He didn't know whether or not he was in the room with others. He didn't know whether or not his hands were bound. But he knew enough to ask these questions to himself.

His mind knew the questions, but it was slow to find the answers.

Everything seemed to be coming at him in a stilted, strange way.

His stomach was painfully empty, and his throat was parched. It had been a long, long time since he'd eaten, or had any water.

Slowly, the events of yesterday came back to him... so much had happened in such a short amount of time.

Slowly, Max began to notice that his hands were bound together with what looked like zip ties. But he wasn't tied to anything. He stood up slowly, falling over once in the process as his stiff muscles were slow to respond. That must have been some blow to the head, but Max was pretty sure that he remembered everything that had happened yesterday. He remembered the road block, and the man pointing the gun at his head.

"You're finally awake," came a voice from somewhere close to him.

"Mandy?" said Max, turning to look.

She was seated against the wall. Her hands were also bound. She didn't look like she'd been injured.

"You all right?" said Max.

She nodded. She looked beyond tired.

"How about you?" she said. "That was some blow to the head."

"I'm fine," said Max, shaking himself a little.

Suddenly, he realized how screwed they were... the Jeep. They were separated from the Jeep, which was not only their means of transportation to the farmhouse, but what housed all of their gear... Max cursed himself for not having gone down fighting. He could have pulled his gun. He could have tried something, anything... Now maybe it was too late.

With both his hands zip tied together, Max felt for his gun in his waistband. But it was gone. His heart sank a little. It really was too late.

But it was never too late. Max knew he had to push on.

"Chad?" he said.

She shook her head.

"I don't know," she said. "They took him somewhere else, I guess."

"What happened? I don't remember anything after they hit me in the head."

"They dragged you and me here," she said. "That's it. That's all I know. I've just been waiting for you to wake up."

"Who are they?"

Mandy shrugged.

"Did you see them?"

"Kind of. It was hard. It was dark. They had flashlights... some lanterns... There were about ten of them, maybe. It was hard to tell. They seemed like regular guys from the town or something... you know, small town people. The way they were talking, it sounded like they were convinced we were Russian spies or something."

Max thought for a moment.

"He was asking me if we were with the Russians, I

think," said Max. "Or the Chinese. I don't remember. My best bet is that they think this EMP was some kind of foreign attack. They're probably just trying to defend their town. That must have been what that crazy roadblock was for…"

"Yeah," said Mandy. "That makes sense. They definitely weren't cops or army or anything. They were really unprofessional. They kept arguing about who was going to do what."

"Hmm," said Max. "Maybe we could use that to our advantage. So there didn't seem to be a leader?"

"Not really," said Mandy. "Maybe a couple of the guys thought they were the leaders. Seemed like they hadn't really worked it out yet." She paused for a moment then added, "I hope Chad's OK."

"He'll be fine," grunted Max. "A little roughing up wouldn't hurt him."

"How's your head?"

"Fine."

Max didn't want to admit it, but it hurt, and it hurt bad. But his memory and thinking seemed to be there, or as there as he could hope for.

His body was running on nothing more than adrenaline, but that false energy was starting to fade. The hunger was there, and it wasn't going to go away, no matter how much adrenaline pumped through his veins.

Standing up, Max examined the zip ties binding his hands. He remembered a video he'd happened to watch once, and did his best to imitate the move that the man in the video had demonstrated.

He held his hands, in fists, above his head. He brought them swiftly down towards his groin area, pulling as hard as he could. As the movement of his body caused his wrists to want to split apart, the zip ties snapped in half with a satisfying noise. He was free.

"How'd you do that?" said Mandy, surprised.

Max didn't answer. Instead, he felt in his pocket for his pocket knife.

"Amateurs," he muttered to himself, realizing that his knife was still there.

He pulled it out, flicked it open, and had Mandy's wrists zip-tie free in seconds.

"Do you know where we are?" he said.

"Looks like the back of some store," said Mandy.

Max looked around carefully for the first time. Indeed, there were all the things you might expect to find in the back of a small town store. There was a broom, a dustpan, some bags of trash that hadn't been thrown out. The place wasn't tidy. There were huge spots of dirt on the floor, and odds and ends scattered all about.

The only artificial light in the place, which of course no longer worked, was a single light bulb hanging by an extension cord that was draped over one of the beams to the roof.

"Hell of a place," said Max. "We've got to get out of here."

"But what are we going to do? They've got guns. They'll catch us for sure. This is a small town. We're not too far from the road block. They didn't take us far... They've got to be all around."

Max shrugged. "I don't know," he said. "Any ideas?"

Mandy was silent.

Max studied her face carefully. In the morning light, she looked different. All night they'd been talking in the car, but he hadn't been able to see her most of the time. It had been as if he'd been talking to a disembodied voice almost.

He saw in her face that she was hungry and tired, but that she had some inner strength, some force that would propel her forward. He hadn't seen that strength in her before.

He also saw that she really was beautiful. There were some minor lines on her face. She hadn't had an easy life. She'd been through some shit. But she had those classically beautiful features that time or worry couldn't touch.

Max was trying to think while he watched Mandy, but no plans came to him. His head still felt fuzzy from the blow.

"The only thing I can think of," said Mandy. "Is that they seem really disorganized. Maybe we can use that to our advantage. You know, convince one of them he should be the leader or something, and then play them off each other?"

"This isn't some comedy movie," said Max. "This shit is real. That'll never work."

"You got a better plan?" said Mandy.

"Someone's coming," whispered Max.

He watched through the morning light in the dusty room as the door handle started to turn.

13

GEORGIA

"That's crazy, Mom," said James.

"Yeah, you've really lost your mind now," said Sadie. "Why can't we just go home?"

"Really, Sadie?" said Georgia. "You think we can just go home?"

Sadie didn't say anything. Georgia knew she was just speaking out, or acting out, or whatever they called it. Sometimes it seemed like teenagers were just as bad as toddlers.

"You can't just go steal some car," said James. "Anyway, I don't see any cars around here."

"A truck," said Georgia, correcting him. "It needs to be a truck or an SUV, or something with four wheel drive."

"Like one of those Subaru wagons?" said Sadie.

"Sadie!" said James. "Don't encourage her."

"Exactly, Sadie," said Georgia.

Her children had been a comfort to her, sitting by her side and telling her that everything would be OK. That was what had given her the strength to pursue this idea.

She was tired and weary. She would need to eat before starting.

"I'm going," she said. "It's the only way. Unless you want to walk all the way there with all our gear."

"We can do it," said James. "We'll just take the food and stuff... we'll be fine."

Georgia considered it for a moment. Actually, he did have a bit of a point.

"It's a long walk," she said.

"But it's better than not getting there at all," said James.

"I don't know," said Georgia. "I don't feel like I'm thinking clearly. Let's get something to eat."

Georgia went to the bed of the damaged pickup and grabbed some tins of food that were stuffed into a paper shopping bag. Everything was so disorganized and there weren't proper bags for most of the stuff. It would be very difficult to carry the gear with them if they did end up walking.

Georgia was too tired to figure out how long it would take to walk there. But it would be days, if not weeks. Actually, she had no idea. She tried to do the math, but she got stuck on wondering about how many miles per hour they would be walking.

"It's cold soup," said Georgia, bringing a couple cans back to her kids. "But it's what we got. I don't want to break out the stove yet. So no complaining, Sadie."

"What?" said Sadie, grabbing the can of soup eagerly. "I don't care if it's cold. I'm starving."

Georgia was too tired to chuckle.

The tops of the cans were the kind that they could peel back easily without using a can opener.

The three of them sat cross-legged facing each other, drinking down their soup. Georgia poured the noodles and beef chunks into her mouth, tipping the can up high.

Nothing had ever tasted so good.

After about ten minutes, she felt better. Not a lot better. She still hadn't slept much. The three of them had fallen asleep in the truck. Georgia had tried to stay awake, and she'd vaguely had the idea of taking shifts to keep guard, but she'd simply been too exhausted, and she'd fallen asleep before she could remember.

"I want another," said James.

"We've got to save it," said Georgia. "We don't know how long it is before we get to the cabin."

"Why can't you just shoot something here, Mom?" said Sadie.

"I thought you didn't approve of hunting," said James.

"I don't want to draw attention to us," said Georgia. "The shot would ring out loud and clear all around. Plus, what am I going to do, field dress a deer and then drag it with us?"

Sadie didn't say anything.

"It's a good idea, though, Sadie," said Georgia, her motherly instincts kicking in. "I'll be teaching you how to hunt soon enough. Once we get to the cabin..."

"So we're walking there, right?" said James.

Despite the soup, Georgia still didn't feel like her energetic self. And she knew that Sadie and James were tired. In the light of day, their faces looked weary.

"Here's what we'll do," said Georgia. "You and Sadie are going to stay here. You're going to stay in the woods, away from the truck..."

"Mom!" said Sadie. "You can't leave us here."

"This is one time that I agree with her," said James.

"Hear me out before you start arguing with me," said Georgia. "Here's what's going to happen. I'm going to hike down the road. If I don't find a house with a car there that I can take, then I'll come back by the end of the day. You two will stay here, in the woods, with guns and food. If anyone comes near the truck to steal anything, shoot them dead."

"Mom!" cried out Sadie.

"You're going to listen to me if you want to survive," said Georgia. "While you're waiting, Sadie, let your brother show you how to shoot, but don't actually fire any shots."

"Are you sure about this, Mom?" said James.

She looked into his eyes and saw that he had that steely determined look that his father had had many years before, before he'd changed his ways and run off. Georgia felt pride swelling in her chest for her son.

"Yes," said Georgia. "We can walk there if I don't find a vehicle, but it's riskier. Our chances of getting there safely in a car are much better."

Georgia started to get ready. She took the pistol and a rifle with her, along with a small bag with some food.

She gave James and Sadie a hug each. Sadie had tears in her eyes when Georgia started walking down the road.

"It's going to be fine, Sadie," said Georgia.

James just looked at her with that determined look.

"I know you'll protect her, James," said Georgia.

James gave her a stiff nod. He understood that this was the best thing, the best course of action. It seemed as if overnight he'd become a man.

Georgia started walking down the road. She tried not to look back, but she couldn't help it.

They were standing there, watching her walk down the road.

The sun had been shining, but clouds were starting to form, obscuring the light. The trees were thick on the sides of the road, which was filled with potholes.

It was a long road ahead, and Georgia didn't know where it would lead. Her feet were already tired and her head hurt from lack of sleep. Her rifle was slung over her shoulder, and her handgun was tucked into the waistband of her jeans.

Her boots hitting the pavement made the only sound in the area.

She turned back once more, looking over at her children, the children she was determined to protect.

14

JAMES

"**M**om's been gone a long time," said Sadie. "Do you think she's OK?"

They were seated in the woods. Sadie had her back against a tall tree, and James sat cross-legged. A rifle lay in his lap. There was one propped up against the tree against which Sadie leaned.

James nodded. "She's probably fine," he said. "You know Mom, she doesn't take shit from anybody."

"Except us," said Sadie.

Maybe she was right.

James didn't want to admit it to his sister, but he was worried. The day was wearing on. He didn't know what time it was, but it was at least mid-afternoon.

The sun wasn't shining brightly. Instead, there were thick clouds that had rolled in slowly throughout the day.

From where they sat, they could see the truck parked on the side of the road. The gear was exposed completely in the bed of the truck. So far, not a single vehicle had driven by. They must have been taking some serious back roads, if not a single car had passed.

James had, throughout the day, turned to his old life. He wondered what had happened to his friends from school, especially his buddy Jimmy, and Mia, the girl he'd been crushing on hard for the last three months... she just had a body that made him go crazy when he looked at her.

He'd spoken to her a few times, but only managed to mutter one or two words, and she'd given him this look like he was an alien or something. But he was getting there... But now he didn't have any idea what Mia or Jimmy's fates would be. For all he knew, the whole area had descended into chaos. Then again, James had probably watched too many zombie movies. Maybe they were all just going to starve to death. Or maybe they were going to wander into the country looking for food... Maybe they'd be eating each other. James didn't know. He wasn't sure that he wanted to know.

James knew that he needed to concentrate on the present. If they were going to survive, he needed to be helping his mom. Sadie had saved the day back at the McKinneys', but now she seemed to be retreating to the role that she was comfortable with, which was mainly whining and complaining.

"I'm hungry," said Sadie, grabbing another can of soup.

The two of them had brought some of the provisions into the woods with them.

"Speak more quietly," said James. "And we need to save that food."

"No one's here," said Sadie. "And I'm hungry. I need my energy."

"You think I'm not hungry?" said James.

"I wish Mom was back," said Sadie.

"Shh," hissed James.

"You're always trying to shut me up," complained Sadie.

"No, serious. I hear something."

Sadie fell silent.

Sure enough, there was a sound coming from somewhere down the road.

"It sounds like an engine," whispered Sadie.

Maybe her hearing was better than James's. It took another ten seconds before he could identity the sound. Sure enough, it did sound like an engine. Someone was driving up the road.

"What do we do?" whispered Sadie. She sounded terrified, and James knew that he had to protect her. And protect the truck and their gear.

He briefly thought of his mother and hoped that she was OK, whatever she was getting herself into. She hadn't proven to be too adept at stealing at the McKinneys', and he hoped she'd learned something from that. What that something was, James had no idea.

It took at least a minute for the vehicle to appear in front of them.

They were seated slightly up above the road, and they both looked down. James was surprised to see that the car was a shiny, new-looking SUV. It was one of those big ones, with darkly tinted windows. He couldn't see inside, but he had an ominous feeling deep in the pit of his stomach.

The SUV stopped right next to the pickup.

But no one got out.

He and Sadie exchanged a look of concern.

Finally, with the engine of the SUV still running, the door opened and the driver got out.

He was a huge man, muscular and fit. He wore a tight t-shirt that showed off his bulging muscles.

No one else got out of the car, but for all James knew, it could have been full of other passengers.

The man looked around him, apparently looking for the owner of the pickup. He seemed to look right at James as he scanned the woods, but he must not have seen him. After all, the brush and leaves were thick, and the man wore dark sunglasses, which wouldn't have helped him see well on the cloudy day.

Sadie was mouthing something at James, and he hoped she wouldn't speak. They were close enough that if she did, the man would certainly hear her. Fortunately, she had enough sense not to. James noticed that she was slowly reaching for her rifle. He had shown her the basics, how to check to make sure it was loaded, how to disengage the safety, how to feel for the catch point on the trigger.

James watched in horror as the muscular man opened the door to his mother's pickup and stuck his head in, apparently looking for something. Next, he got out and started poking around in the bed.

The muscular man grabbed a couple shopping bags of food, walked calmly towards his on SUV, popped the automatic rear door, and started loading the food into it.

"He's going to steal everything," whispered Sadie in the quietest voice James had ever heard. But he understood her, and the sound of the shopping bags rustling must have been enough to cover the whisper.

James had to act. And he had to act soon. His job was to protect his family, and that meant protecting their food and their supplies. He couldn't let some stranger simply rob them.

James clutched his rifle tightly, but he didn't yet bring it into firing position. His heart rate had skyrocketed. He was breathing heavily. He didn't know what to do, but he knew what he *had* to do.

15

CHAD

Chad was in a sweaty daze, yet he was also on edge. It had been hours since he'd taken his last Vicodin, and he was not enjoying the withdrawal effects one bit. He'd been through this before, when he'd tried to clean up. It hadn't gone well. He'd ended up destroying half his apartment in an angry rage, screaming at his landlord, and perhaps throwing a cat somewhere, not that he could really remember much of it.

The pills were in Max's Jeep. Chad cursed himself for leaving them there, but he was always letting stuff accidentally fall out of his pockets, so he'd stuffed the pills in that seat pocket behind Max's seat.

Not that he could have gotten the pills anyway.

His hands were bound with something, and he lay on his side on the dirty floor in an uncomfortable position. But he was too far into the withdrawal to care about it.

Some of the men who'd dragged them from the Jeep were seated nearby. They sat in lawn chairs around a dying fire, discussing something in low voices.

They'd grilled him practically all night, asking him

repeatedly who he worked for. Chad didn't know where Max and Mandy were, or what had happened to them.

Chad was scared, worried, and confused. But a lot of that fear didn't have to do with these men. As the night had worn on, it had become clear that these men were just some regular guys from a small town. They were scared that everything had turned off, that there was no power and no communications. They were in the same situation everyone else was in, except that they were in a small town. And so they feared the worst—some kind of foreign government takeover.

One of them got lazily up from his lawn chair. "I'll go interrogate him some more," he said sleepily and half-heartedly.

He walked slowly over to Chad, who watched his dirty boots as they came closer to him.

"So," said the man. "You say you're not with the Russians, or the Chinese... So who are you with?"

"Come on, man," said Chad. "I'm an American, just like you. I'm from Pennsylvania. Born and raised."

He'd been over this a thousand times. He didn't have the patience for it anymore, despite his position as a prisoner.

"That so?" said the man lazily, his mouth full of chewing tobacco. He spat onto the ground in front of him, and rubbed the ground with his boot, digging the toe into the soil.

"This is bullshit," said Chad. "Where'd you take my friends?"

"They're fine," said the man.

Chad got the sense that these men didn't want to hurt them.

"I get it, man," said Chad. "You're just scared. We all are. But we've got to learn to work together on this."

"How's that?"

"The way I see it," said Chad. "It'd be a lot better for you guys if you just let us all go. You could concentrate on doing shit you actually need to do, like finding food, that sort of thing... You can't be spending all your time essentially working as prison guards... This is just crazy."

"You watch your mouth."

"He giving you any trouble?" called one of the men from the campfire.

"Nah, he's fine."

"Listen," said another man around the campfire. "I got to get going. Sally's going to be worried sick about me."

"The old ball and chain," muttered someone else. "Our country's been attacked and she won't even let you stay out all night. Doesn't she know there are some things worth fighting for?"

"I don't see us doing a hell of a lot of fighting."

Chad had had enough of it all.

"Shut up!" he screamed, at the top of his drug-deprived lungs.

The men were all stunned into silence.

"You obviously have no idea what you're even doing!" shouted Chad. "You don't even know how to interrogate me properly. Now I say either let me and my friends go, right now. That's option one, OK?" He wasn't sure he was completely making sense, but he was too far gone and too frustrated to care. "Option two is you go get me my damn pills right now. OK? Option three is that you just torture me already, because I've had enough of this shit."

The men didn't know what to do. They were all standing in front of him now, staring at this strange prisoner who'd just screamed at them. They shifted their weight. They spat their tobacco juice.

"You know," said one of them. "Maybe he's got a point. We didn't really torture him."

"Come on, we're not like that. Plus, Sally would kill me if she knew I was out here torturing people."

"Desperate times call for desperate measures. If you can't handle it, then head home."

"Just kill me," shouted Chad.

The last thing he remembered was a boot coming towards him, right towards his face. He lost consciousness quickly. If he had been conscious of what was happening, he would have been happy to pass out. It was better than the reality of the withdrawal he was experiencing.

Georgia had walked for hours. There hadn't been any houses, or any cars passing by. She was about to give up and turn around. After all, she'd told James and Sadie that she would be back before the end of the day. She was weary and tired and she didn't feel as if she was completely thinking clearly. But at least she was cognizant of that fact, and would be able to take precautions against making rash decisions. All she needed to do was double check the decisions she was making. She would need to pause and reconsider something that would have otherwise been an obvious decision. That was something she'd learned being out in the woods for days on end in her younger years.

The sky was dense with grey, ominous clouds. But so far there was no rain.

The air was cool out here, whereas in the suburbs it had been sweltering hot, as spring was growing into a scorching summer.

Georgia sat down on the side of the road to think again about returning. Should she press on farther? She didn't have a watch, and obviously her cell phone wasn't working.

For the first time, Georgia heard the sounds of birds around her. They'd been strangely absent all along this journey. Then again, she'd been concentrating on other things, and hadn't exactly had time to listen to the birds chirp.

Georgia's mind turned towards the situation as a whole. Again she wondered whether this was a localized event. She was pretty sure that it was not. For instance, if part of Pennsylvania experienced a complete blackout, or an EMP, then surely the rest of the country would come to their aid. The national guard would be sent in, and there would be volunteers showing up by the truckload. Nothing like that was happening. If it had been the entire United States, then foreigners were about to show up. Georgia didn't know if they'd be invading soldiers, or peacekeepers coming to help.

Georgia was cynical in a lot of ways. She didn't expect foreign peacekeepers to show up to help. She expected soldiers, and she expected them quickly.

So the only logical conclusion was that the entire planet had been affected...

That must mean that it was some kind of natural event, like a solar flare, rather than something artificial... Nothing Georgia knew about could have that kind of worldwide range.

Then again, Georgia realize she was tired and she was getting a little ahead of herself. There was no way she could determine what had happened all over the entire world. Not while she was alone on a remote rural road, with no cell phone, no internet, no communications whatsoever.

Georgia decided to give it another ten minutes.

And she was glad she did.

She had to convince her tired feet to move, one step at a

time. But at the top of a long, sloping hill, she saw something.

At first, all she saw was a streak of pink against the background of the forest. The house was so far in the distance that she had to keep walking for some time before she could clearly make out that it was a house. It looked so small in the distance.

When she got closer, she saw that there was a small compact car parked in the driveway. Obviously, no lights were on in the house.

Georgia took a deep breath before continuing onward. Her shoulder was sore from carrying the rifle. Her feet hurt even more. She knew she would have been able to tolerate all this if she was better rested and better fed. But when food and sleep start lacking, everything else gets much, much harder.

It took Georgia what must have been at least another half an hour to walk to the house. She left the road and walked through the woods, which made the distance longer and the path harder. But she wanted to make sure she wasn't seen.

Georgia didn't know what the odds would be that someone was in the house.

She took the rifle from her shoulder and held it in her hands, ready to use it if needed.

Georgia didn't want to kill. Especially not when she was the one robbing someone else. She would kill to defend herself or her kids. But when she was out on the prowl? Could she justify that to herself? She knew that they needed a vehicle... but could she really do it?

I'll just have to cross that path when I get to it, thought Georgia. But she realized that that was a dangerous proposition, and she promised herself that she would do everything she could not to kill another human being... unless the person was threatening her... Then she would have to do what she had to do.

Hiding behind a tree and peeking out from it, she studied the car. It certainly wasn't an SUV, a truck, or anything with four wheel drive. It was a small compact car, made in Japan.

It might have been a Honda or Nissan, or even an ancient Datsun, but it looked like the markings might have been taken off, and Georgia wasn't that familiar with those types of cars.

It would do, though. It would at least get her and her family and most of their gear near the hunting cabin. They would have to walk the rest of the way. With this small compact car, she'd be able to take much more gear to the cabin than if they went the whole way on foot. In Georgia's mind, more gear meant a higher chance of surviving.

Georgia crept forward, practically holding her breath. She used the movements that she'd learned in the woods, the ones that didn't scare animals. She moved steadily, making little noise.

She figured the best thing to do was just see if the car had a spare key there, or if by some strange stroke of luck, the key was still in the ignition.

Georgia kept one eye on the house at all times. She was crouched down next to the car, the rifle held in one hand. Her other hand felt underneath the wheel wells. She moved around to each wheel, and tried the bumpers.

No luck.

She tried the doors to the car, but they were locked. She broke her gaze from the house for a moment to examine the car, putting a hand above her eyes to shield her view from the glare. It didn't look like a key was in there. Who left their keys in the car, anyway?

Georgia considered her options again. She didn't have any idea how to hotwire cars. Although this car was older, and maybe she could jam a screwdriver into the ignition or something. Foolishly, she didn't have a screwdriver with her, or even a multitool. But anyway, that might take some time, and the owner of the car, if he or she was home, was bound to come out.

The best thing to do, Georgia realized, was simply confront the problem head on. She wanted to steal this car? Then she needed to simply head into the house, point her gun at the owner, and take the keys from them under threat of violence.

Georgia didn't like it one bit. But she was doing it for her family.

What were the chances that the owner of the home had a gun? Maybe 50%, thought Georgia, considering it was a more rural area.

Georgia was going to take her chances.

If something happened to her, if she was shot, then James and Sadie still had the map. They would be able to reach the cabin, and continue their life from there on out. Or so Georgia hoped. She hoped with all her heart that they were OK right now.

She'd never been a very sentimental person, but that didn't mean she didn't care about her kids. And she was realizing now that she cared for them more deeply than she'd thought possible.

Georgia walked to the back of the house slowly. Still no sign of anyone living in it.

There was a big panel of windows on the back. Georgia

walked slowly towards them and peered through. She just saw a darkened kitchen.

Georgia wasn't going to try to break in again. Not if someone was home. She knocked loudly on the backdoor, hammering her fist against the glass. The area was so quiet, with all the machines off, no air conditioner blowing, no fans, that there was no way someone wouldn't hear her if they were home.

Georgia slung the rifle back over her shoulder and grabbed the handgun. She stood off to the side, pressing her body against the siding of the house. No one would be able to see her.

After a couple minutes, nothing had happened. No one came to the door.

Someone might be in there. Someone might be waiting with a gun drawn, ready to shoot her if she tried to enter.

But she was going to take the risk.

She was going to have to break the window.

Well, she might as well try the door first.

To her complete and utter surprise, the door was open.

It could be a trap.

But she had to go in.

She slid the door open, and then held her gun forward, walking behind it. She turned the corner carefully, leading the way with the gun.

"Anyone here?" she called out loudly.

She figured it was better to announce her presence. If someone was waiting for her in hiding, they already knew she was here.

She paused in the kitchen and waited. She crouched down and steadied the gun with her other hand. She pointed it at the entrance to what must have been the main downstairs hallway. She'd closed the door behind her, so that if someone was outside, they would have to open the door to shoot her. The glass was thick, and a bullet might not go through it. At the very least, it was some form of protection.

After a long time, Georgia had heard nothing in the house. There wasn't a single sign that someone was here.

That didn't mean someone wasn't waiting, knife drawn, or gun pointed.

But she had to take her chances.

She found herself holding her breath as she moved through the house, gun drawn, finger inside the trigger guard.

She found the keys in a little porcelain bowl on a table by the front door.

She considered searching the house for other goods, but realized that she was already going to be downsizing when she got back to the truck.

Georgia felt a thrill, a complete rush of relief, as she went back outside and unlocked the car.

It started up fine, the little engine purring quietly. There was practically nothing in the car, and it was immaculately clean.

Georgia didn't have time to ponder her good luck. She backed out of the driveway, and started driving back the way she came.

The car was automatic, so there wasn't any point in putting it in neutral. She let out a whoop as she let it coast down the hill, heading back towards the pickup and, more importantly, James and Sadie.

As she was rolling down the hill, something appeared in her peripheral vision. There were three people walking along the side of the road.

Their jaws dropped as they saw Georgia driving along in

the car. She saw the recognition on their faces, and knew instantly it was their car.

It wasn't a family. They were three middle aged women. They couldn't have been much older than Georgia herself. They looked tired and weary, and their faces fell in despair as they realized that their car was gone, and that Georgia was taking it from them.

They weren't armed.

Instead of shooting, they started waving their hands wildly, as if Georgia had done the deed somehow by mistake. As if she would realize her error, stop the car, and give it back to them.

Mandy stood frozen as the door opened. A man entered, and Max immediately sprang towards him. Max grabbed the man by the waist and pushed with all his weight.

The two of them crashed into the wall. The man grunted, and Max cried out in pain as the man did something to his arm.

Mandy couldn't see what had happened. The two were a flurry of bodies.

The next thing she knew, it was all over too fast. Max was bashing his elbow repeatedly into the man's stomach.

The man fell down, gasping for breath.

Max was holding his wrist in a funny way, as if it was injured. He looked down at the man.

The man started to move.

"Don't move," said Max.

The man moved anyway, lunging out towards Max.

Max kicked him in the stomach.

"Stay down," he muttered.

The man twitched. Max gave him another swift kick.

"Max!" cried out Mandy.

"What do you want me to do?" said Max. "Bake him a birthday cake?"

Mandy saw that he had a point. After all, the man had kidnapped them and imprisoned them in this room. He didn't deserve any special treatment.

Max wasn't being cruel about it. Once the man had stopped moving, Max had stopped too. He wasn't attacking him out of cruelty or enjoyment. It was survival, pure and simple.

"What are we going to do?" said Mandy.

"Got any ideas?" said Max. "Because I'm all out of them."

"How's your wrist?"

"Fine," said Max.

But it didn't look fine.

He bent down and examined the man. He took the rffle that was slung over the man's shoulders. He tried to hold up the sight to his eye to examine it. Or maybe he was examining the barrel. Mandy wasn't sure. She didn't know much about guns. To her, a rifle was a rifle. A handgun was a handgun, whatever type it was.

"Here," said Max, wincing in pain as he handed her the rifle.

Mandy took it gingerly. "Um, shouldn't you carry it?"

"My wrist," said Max. "I can't work the gun."

"I don't even know how to use it."

"It's not that hard. Point and shoot, basically."

"Basically?"

"Let's go," said Max.

"Go? Go where? If we go out there... there are a ton of people out there..."

"We're going to have to risk it," said Max.

He walked right out into the day through the doorway.

The light seemed to illuminate him completely, even though it was cloudy. Mandy followed him and the brightness of the light surprised her.

The trees were all around them. They had never looked so beautiful. It had been a long time since Mandy had been out in nature. All last night had been dark, very dark, and she hadn't gotten a look past the magnificence of the majestic trees.

"You see anyone?" said Max in a low voice.

Mandy shook her head.

They were out back behind the store.

"Maybe everyone's inside," said Mandy. "I bet they're terrified."

"Look over there," said Max, pointing with his good hand. "A fire."

Suddenly, they heard yelling.

"Look," said Mandy, as they started jogging towards the fire. They could now see a group of figures around a man lying on the ground.

"I bet that's Chad."

Mandy didn't know why they were running right towards a group of men with guns. She'd just moved automatically, perhaps sensing that it might be Chad.

But why was she trying to protect Chad? She didn't even know him. And so far, he'd seemed more like a liability than anything else.

Max was running faster than she was. He had long legs, and good form. He ran easily across the slightly muddy field.

Mandy struggled to keep up, holding the rifle in both hands in front of her.

It started to dawn on her that this was a really bad idea. These men were dangerous. They were armed.

Up ahead, she saw one of them kick Chad in the stomach. Chad went limp.

What the hell was Max planning on doing when he got up there?

She found out soon enough.

"Hey!" yelled Max, waving his good arm.

"The prisoners!" shouted one of them.

"Stay back, Mandy," yelled Max.

Mandy stopped in her tracks, doing as she was told. She held the gun dumbly, not raising it to a position from which she could fire it.

Was Max crazy? Normally he seemed intent on making the most practical decisions, decisions that would save his own hide.

But with Chad, it was different. For Chad, he'd risked their lives back at that mob. For Chad, he was rushing towards a group of armed men.

She hoped he knew what he was doing.

There were four men. Each now pointed a handgun at Max.

One looked at Mandy, and trained his gun on her instead.

Max was only about ten feet from them. Mandy was behind, but easily within ear shot.

Max held up his hands to show that he wasn't armed.

The men didn't speak.

"Listen," said Max, firmly frozen in place. "We didn't come here to harm you. We're just like you... Confused and scared."

"We're not scared of nothing," said one of men.

Another grunted in agreement.

The other two didn't seem so sure.

"We're not with any foreign government," said Max. "If

you didn't notice, we have American accents just like you. I'm from nearby. I grew up right outside Philly."

"That's just what a spy would say."

"Listen," said Max. "I don't care what you fellows think. Because I already know exactly what you're going to do. And I'm going to tell you what that is, in clear and simple language so that you can follow along."

"Looks like you're not the one in the bargaining position."

"That's what it would look like, yes," said Max. "To an untrained eye. But what you don't realize is that you're the ones in danger right now."

"How's that?"

Max didn't say anything for quite a while.

Mandy had the distinct feeling that Max hadn't yet thought of what to say. He was thinking on his feet.

"OK," said Max. "That lady back there. You see her? She's not what she appears. She's not just some ordinary girl. She's a highly trained marksman, or I guess they say markswoman now. Whatever. She can take you all out before you have time to pull the trigger."

Mandy groaned internally. She was sure that this wouldn't work.

But to try to make Max's lie more convincing, she raised the gun, putting her eye to the scope the way she'd seen people do in the movies. She pointed the gun at one of the men and hoped she was doing it convincingly. She put her finger on the trigger, but made sure to keep from applying any pressure. She didn't want to shoot anyone by mistake.

"You see," said Max. "You actually did catch some spies. We're nothing but the best. The best spies, that is."

Mandy had the feeling that Max wasn't used to lying. But she had to admit it wasn't that bad of a plan. These guys were so terrified of spies that just maybe it would... maybe. But Max didn't sound too sure of himself. He did, in a way, but he was pausing a lot when speaking.

"Yup," said Max, again. "We're spies... The best... And she's the best sharpshooter..." He was starting to repeat himself.

The guys were looking at each other questioningly.

Mandy knew she had to do something.

"Listen up," shouted Mandy. "Drop the weapons now. Or I open fire. I guarantee I'll take out three of the four of you before you can get off a shot."

Mandy didn't want to make it sound too unrealistic. She had no idea if it was possible to shoot three people before they shot her, but in her mind three sounded better than four. That just sounded too boastful and unrealistic.

Were they going to buy it?

They didn't look too smart. They had dumb looking faces and confused expressions.

Mandy wished she knew how to do that thing with a gun that made that noise, the thing they were always doing in movies. Cocking the gun? She wasn't sure. This wasn't that type of gun. Maybe there was a bolt somewhere. But she couldn't exactly go groping around with her hand looking for a bolt.

Chad started groaning from down on the ground.

"Aw, shit, man," he said, loudly. He sounded as if he was in pain.

The moments were dragging on. Mandy didn't know what to do.

"That's it!" she cried out. She felt like the best strategy was simply to be completely overconfident. "You're all going down."

She moved her body, pretending that she was adjusting

the way the rifle sat on her shoulder. She moved her trigger finger around a little, hoping they could see it moving, hoping that it was twitching or something.

"Ok!" shouted one of the men. He started lowering his gun to the ground.

"Drop it!" shouted Mandy.

"What are you doing?" said his buddy.

"Dude, she's going to kill us."

"How do you know that?"

"You were the one who said they were spies in the first place."

"Drop it," shouted Mandy.

The man dropped his gun to the ground.

Mandy held her breath as it fell, hoping that it wouldn't fire as it hit the ground. In truth, she didn't know if that actually happened, but she was pretty sure she'd seen it in a movie somewhere.

The other men followed suit.

Mandy held her gun on them, as if she knew how to fire it.

Max walked forward and picked up the guns. He examined them. She saw him open one of the guns and check for bullets. It was a revolver, she thought. The other guns looked different, more modern.

Max stuck one in his waistband and one in his pocket. He held another awkwardly with his good hand and pointed it at the men.

"How you doing, Chad?" said Max.

"Awful," said Chad, loudly, nearly shouting. "They took my damn meds from me."

"What are you taking?" said Mandy.

"Vicodin," muttered Chad. He sounded as if he was in serious withdrawal.

Mandy could see it in Chad's face. He was suffering. But she didn't have much sympathy for him. He'd enjoyed the highs, and now he had to deal with the lows.

"Great," said Mandy. "I told you, Max. He's on serious shit."

Max didn't answer her.

The men were looking at each other. They looked terrified.

"Get down on your knees," shouted Mandy.

They did as they were told, sinking their knees into the mud.

"Please don't kill us," said one.

"Yeah," said the other. "You know, I've always been a big fan of hockey. I hear that's big in Russia..."

"So you're a traitor, are you?" said his buddy.

"No, it's not like that. I'm just saying if they're taking over, then I might as well get with the new sports. They're going to need Americans to run their Russian hockey leagues or whatever."

"Idiots," said Max. "You think we're really Russians or something?"

"You're not?"

"I told you that from the beginning. But don't get any funny ideas. That doesn't mean she isn't one hell of a shot. And we're more than willing to shoot you. Now where's the Jeep you stole from me?"

"Right where it was before."

"You idiots didn't even move it? Is everything still in it?"

All the men nodded.

"Amateurs," muttered Max, more to himself than to anyone else.

"All right," said Max, to Mandy and Chad. "Looks like

this pleasant little detour is over. Let's get the hell out of here."

Chad managed to get himself off the ground. His over-sized body was covered in mud, both dried and wet. His hair was matted. He looked terrible. His face had gone all blotchy, and it was puffy yet gaunt at the same time.

"See you... Jeep..." said Chad, not really paying any attention to them.

He rushed off as fast as he could across the field, headed towards the Jeep, towards his pills.

"I guess he's going to get his pills," said Mandy coldly.

"Come on," said Max. "Let's go."

"Wait," said Mandy. "I've got a few more questions for these idiots."

"What could you possibly want to ask them?"

"Don't we need information? We haven't talked to anyone else. I want to know what the hell's going on."

"What's going on? Everything is broken. Nothing works. Society is collapsing. That's what's going on."

"I want to hear it from them." She still had her gun trained on them, even as Max was starting to walk away.

"So," she said to them. "Tell me what you know."

Max paused and looked back.

"They don't know anything," he said. "They're idiots. They thought we were Russian spies."

"What do you know?" repeated Mandy.

"Honestly, nothing," said one. He seemed to be the smartest of the group. "Nobody's come through here. We figured the US had been attacked."

"Hmm," said Mandy. "Quite the astute conclusion."

They didn't seem to know what that meant.

"Where's everyone else in this town?" said Mandy.

"At home. Everyone's hiding."

"Then what are you men doing out?"

"Well, there's no sheriff. He died a month ago from a heart attack, and I guess we never got around to getting a new one."

"So what are you saying?"

"Well we just went ahead and deputized each other, I suppose. That way we're responsible for the safety of these parts."

"Are you all just idiots or something?" said Max.

Mandy didn't say anything at first. But a thought came to her.

"And how's everyone doing?" she said. "Is everyone all right?"

"Is everyone all right?" said Max. "Are you crazy? Come on, let's get out of this podunk town. We've got places to go and things to do. And I'm starving."

Mandy looked at the men. One of them wore an uncomfortable expression that she couldn't quite read.

She'd always had a good read on people, and truthfully she knew that despite her own anger, these men had just been trying to protect themselves and more importantly their families. They'd assumed the worst, which wasn't really that far off—or it might not have been. After all, Mandy and Max had no idea what had happened.

Mandy knew that these weren't cruel men. Not deep in their hearts. They didn't want to hurt Mandy, Max, or Chad, despite what they'd already done.

And something was wrong. She could see it in the man's sad face.

"Who is it?" said Mandy, looking directly at him. She lowered her gun, pointing the muzzle at the ground. "Who's sick?"

"Who's sick?" said Max. "Are you crazy? Come on, let's get out of here."

"It's my dad," said the man, who noticed that Mandy had lowered her gun. "I don't know what's wrong with him, but he's not right."

The other men lowered their heads in sadness.

"He was on dialysis... We were taking him down to Philly twice a week. Obviously that's not possible now..."

"That's a long drive," said Mandy. "Come on, take me to your father. Maybe we can help."

They men looked at each other hesitantly.

"Come on," said Mandy, waving her arm. "Take me to him. Come on!"

They got up slowly and started to walk towards her.

Max walked back to her. "What are you doing?" he hissed in her ear. "Don't you remember what they just did to us? Now the guy supposedly has a sick dad that you want to help?"

18

JAMES

"You've got to do something," hissed Sadie in his ear.

James had the scope of the gun to his eye.

His finger was on the trigger, but he couldn't bring himself to shoot. That wasn't right. He had to speak first, but he was terrified.

And worst of all, his mother had counted on him. Counted on him to protect himself, Sadie, and the possessions. Without the gear, they were screwed, and James knew that well. He understood the gravity of the situation. Even Sadie did now. She'd stopped checking her dead phone every five minutes.

While James was sweating, while his heart was pounding, the man was quickly loading gear into his SUV.

"You need to do something," hissed Sadie, again.

James knew she was right.

"Stop right there," he cried out.

The man froze. He was on the way back to the pickup, his arms empty.

"Who's out there?" he called out.

"Don't move a muscle," shouted James. He made an attempt to make his voice sound deeper and more manly that it might have otherwise been. Not that he wasn't a man, but he didn't always sound like one.

"Who's out there?" shouted the man.

He moved his sunglasses up to get a better look. He started peering right where James and Sadie were hiding, but James was pretty sure he wasn't seen.

"Who's out there?" shouted the man again.

To James's horror, the man didn't sound scared. He didn't *look* scared. His posture was relaxed.

He was one of those huge muscular gym rats, who wasn't intimidated by anyone.

"I've got a gun trained on you," shouted James. "And I won't hesitate to shoot you in the head. Return what you've taken, and leave. If you don't want to die."

James hoped that sounded convincing enough.

To his horror, the man started to laugh to himself.

"So you're some kid out there in the woods? You've got your dad's hunting rifle, is that it?"

James didn't know what to say. He didn't answer.

"How old are you, anyway?" shouted the man. "Twelve? Thirteen?"

James was feeling anxiety and anger rising in his chest. He was far older, and the man knew it, but he was just trying to talk down to him, trying to switch the power dyanmic. But even though James was smart enough to recognize that, he felt powerless to stop it. After all, he wasn't an adult. He didn't know how to talk like one.

"Look, kid," said the man. "I was a cop. Fifteen years on the force. I've seen shit you wouldn't imagine. I've shot guys. I've been shot, too, twice. I worked in the city. I've seen shit you wouldn't believe. Now if you think you're going to scare me with some line about blowing my head off..." He started laughing again. "Just forget it. Just forget it."

The man started walking towards the bed of the truck casually. He peered inside, taking his time examining the provisions, deciding what he wanted to take. He was doing it very obviously. Apparently he wanted James to truly understand who had the power here, making it less likely that James would shoot him.

"Don't move!" shouted James, anger starting to overtake the anxiety. His face felt red and hot. His chest felt full of the anger, which was coursing through him.

But James had enough sense not to just haul off and shoot the guy right there because he was a dick, and because he was angry.

"Look, kid," said the man. "I don't doubt you've got a gun. But come on, have you ever shot someone before? Are you really prepared to shoot at me, miss, and then hit me with your second shot? And watch me bleed out in agony on the pavement? I don't think you're ready for that reality, and I think you won't be able to shoot me. I could easily rush you right now, and you'd be too much of a pussy to even fire a single shot... I could take that gun from you and turn it on you."

"I thought he was a cop," whispered Sadie.

Sadie was more innocent than James. In her world, all cops were good guys.

James knew that they weren't all bad guys, but that sometimes things were more complicated than they seemed. He knew that extreme situations pushed people into new roles. And he knew that some cops were dicks. He and his friends had been harassed and taken down to the station once when they were visiting West Philly on a Friday, just because they'd gone to some punk show.

James had to say something, but he didn't know what.

Why couldn't his mom be there?

But he was a man.

He didn't need his mom to protect him and his sister, and their stuff.

"I may be younger," shouted James. "But this shit won't work. I'm telling you, I'm going to shoot."

The man just laughed and grabbed a couple items from the bed of the pickup.

"You don't have it in you, kid," said the man.

James's instincts were telling him to shoot now. His anger was telling him to shoot. It was his mind that was telling him not to, but now it was swinging around. They needed that stuff.

"Just cause the power's off, doesn't mean you're going to shoot an ex-cop."

The man has his back to James and Sadie. For all James knew, the man might get in his car and drive away, never to be seen again. James thought of how much they needed those provisions, of the long days ahead when times would be tough... What if someone got injured, and Sadie or his mom got hurt?

James pulled the trigger.

His aim was good. The bullet struck the man in the back of the head. His body crumpled to the ground with a sickening thud.

The bags of groceries he'd been holding fell to the ground, making a clattering noise on the pavement.

James instantly felt sick. His blood felt hot.

"Holy shit," said Sadie.

The scene was eerie. The SUV was still running.

Shit, what had he just done?

But he knew he had to be a man about this.

"Stay there," he told Sadie. "There might be someone else in that car. Keep your gun up like this."

He moved her hands and her rifle so that she was holding it properly.

"If you need to, aim it and pull the trigger," said James.

Sadie looked scared, terrified. The reality was hitting her.

James had never killed someone before, let alone seen a dead body.

He started walking through the woods down to the road, moving carefully. Part of his mind was focused on his footing, just some trivial practical thing. The other part of his mind was reeling from what he'd just done. He'd taken a life. He'd killed a man.

As James got closer, he saw the body more clearly.

He leaned over and puked. There wasn't much in his stomach, but whatever it was, it came up, vile and nasty. He could already smell the puke.

But as soon as he vomited, he felt better.

He walked slowly towards the body. There wasn't any need to see if he was dead. He definitely was, his brains splattered on the pavement. It was just like those horrible pictures James had seen on the internet.

James peered into the car. He was a little too dazed and shocked from the experience to lead with his gun.

But there was no one in the car. James double-checked the back, in case someone was hiding there.

James looked up and down the long stretch of empty road under the grey cloudy sky. There was no one.

Where was his mom?

James opened the driver's door, got in, and parked the SUV in front of the pickup. He had to maneuver around the man's dead body. He didn't want to add insult to injury (or death, rather) by squashing the man's body.

He killed the engine and got out.

He grabbed the bags of groceries from the backseat and walked towards the pickup. Then he stopped, realizing that the pickup didn't work.

It suddenly hit him and he felt like an idiot. Now they had a car.

He put the groceries back.

"Sadie!" he called out, gesturing for her to come down. "It's safe. There's no one here."

"Mom told us to stay in the woods," called back Sadie.

"I know, I know, but come down! I need your help with something!"

"I'm not going down there," shouted Sadie.

Sighing, James walked back to her. It seemed to take forever. Time seemed to be slowing down. He wondered if it was the adrenaline. He had to step over the dead man's body, and when he walked along the grass, he saw that there was blood on the bottom of his shoe from the pavement.

Sadie looked completely terrified. She looked exhausted. And hungry.

"He's dead?" said Sadie. She knew he was dead. She definitely already knew.

James nodded. "I didn't have a choice."

"I know," said Sadie quietly.

"Sadie," said James, crouching down in front of her. "I know Mom told us to stay up here. But we've got to make a decision."

"What decision?"

"Well, we've got a working car now. Four wheel drive, everything we need."

"So?"

"So I think we maybe should go drive and look for Mom."

"Are you crazy? She told us to stay here."

"I know, I know. But look, it's getting late. And the clouds look darker. I think it might rain, or even storm."

"We can't just leave," said Sadie. "Mom's going to be coming back to look for us. What happens when she comes back and we're not here?"

"I know, but I thought of that. But look at it this way. We know Mom's going to be coming back down from the direction she came. Either a car or on foot. We'll see her if we drive that way. Right?"

"Yeah," said Sadie. "But what if she doesn't find a car and she takes a shortcut through the woods. You know she'll find a way to do that, if it saves time. She isn't going to be expecting that we're driving. She isn't going to expect us to have a car. What if she walks in the woods along the road?"

James paused, considering it. Sadie had a good point, and he knew it.

"So what do we do?" said James.

"I don't know."

"We could leave a note," said James, looking up at the sky. "I really think it's going to rain. I mean, do you really think Mom is going to find a car that she can steal?"

"That doesn't sound like her," said Sadie. "I mean she's never stolen anything in her life."

"Except that gas."

"Well that was you."

"Shut up."

"I'm worried about her," said Sadie. "None of us have eaten much."

"I'm starting to wonder what the point of bringing all that food was," said James.

"I think we should drive and find her," said Sadie. "We'll leave a note here for her, then if we don't find her, we'll come back."

"The note will say just to wait for us here?"

"Exactly."

"OK," said James. "Let's go."

He helped Sadie to her feet. It seemed as if her legs had fallen asleep.

"James," said Sadie.

"What?"

"I want you to know... I know you had to do it."

She was referring to killing the guy.

James didn't say anything.

"Help me load up the SUV," he said.

They got to work. It was tiring. There was a lot of stuff in the back of the pickup.

But fortunately, the SUV was not only state of the art and apparently brand new, but it was spacious as well. Everything easily fit in there.

Sadie made a sign out of a piece of scrap metal that had been lying in the bottom of the bed of the pickup since James could remember. She used a multitool to carve a message in there.

She propped it up against a rock.

"You think she'll see it?"

"Definitely, and it's good because if someone's just driving by they won't notice it. It'll just look like a piece of metal."

"What if Mom drives by and doesn't see it?"

"She'll stop and look for us. Plus, we'll see her driving down, right? There's only one road."

"As far as we know."

They were ready. James started the car, and the engine

hummed magnificently. It really was a fine vehicle, thought James to himself.

He didn't look back at the dead man on the road. There was no need to. He'd seen all he needed to see. It was death, final and simple. That was it. There wasn't much to it. It wasn't complicated.

The rain was starting to fall as James pulled onto the road. The clouds looked ominous in front of them.

Neither of them spoke. They were both worried. But they were doing what they thought was right. They were convinced they were making the best decision for their family.

19

GEORGIA

eorgia must not have slept as much as she'd thought. Wait, had she slept at all? She was starting to feel delirious from lack of sleep, from hunger, from the fatigue of walking all day.

She'd cruised right past the people whose car she was obviously driving. She wasn't going to stop, not when the well-being of her family was at stake. But she felt a horrible nagging guilt that she hadn't felt in a long time. Those women had looked so... helpless. They'd looked innocent. And she'd seen it on their faces. They simply couldn't believe their bad luck.

She tried to justify it to herself. Where did they need to go in a car anyway? They already had their house.

But soon she was second guessing her own rationalizations.

Well, the house hadn't appeared to have a lot of food in it. Maybe they didn't have much food left, and they would need to leave to get some.

But where were they going to get food? It wasn't like they'd be able to just drive to a grocery store. Even if there was one nearby, it would have been looted long ago. What's more, it would be dangerous.

The sky was a dark grey. The rain started falling. It was light at first, but after only a few minutes, it turned into an intense heavy downpour.

So far, no lightning or thunder. But it really felt like a storm was developing. A heavy, intense storm.

The road didn't have good drainage. Instead of being formed like a crown, sloping down on the sides, it was the reverse of that. The road was shaped like a U, so that water quickly accumulated in the center of it.

Some parts of the road were already flooded.

Georgia had driven trucks as long as she could remember, and she didn't feel confident in the abilities of this little foreign compact car.

Maybe she should have gone looking for a better car, a truck or something. But she knew there were few houses around here. She would have had to walk perhaps an entire extra day.

She was worried about Sadie and James. She hoped nothing had happened to them. She hoped no one had come along to do them harm.

Georgia was going down a long and steep descent. There was a curve coming up ahead, and she slowed down a little. But maybe not enough. After all, she was anxious to get back to James and Sadie.

It happened fast. Maybe it was the water. Or maybe Georgia was driving too fast on the curve.

But the next thing she knew, the car lost control.

Shitty ass tires, was the last thought she had, before the car left the road completely and hit a tree.

The impact wasn't that hard. Surprisingly soft, actually. But she felt jolted, and a little dazed.

The airbag deployed perfectly, just as it should have. It worked beautifully, cushioning what would have been a nasty bashing against the steering wheel.

The engine still running, Georgia tried her seatbelt. But it was jammed.

She knew what was happening, despite being dazed. She didn't stop and cry. She didn't give up. She didn't feel sorry for herself.

Instead, she did what she had to do. She was slowly able to fish her pocket knife from her jeans. She flicked it open, cut the seatbelt, and then punctured the airbag for good measure, allowing her to get out of the car easily.

She stood, slightly dazed, next to the car. It didn't look like there was any way the car would be able to get out of there on its own. She didn't think that it was severely damaged, but it was definitely stuck.

She got back in and put the car in reverse. But the wheels just spun. Yeah, she'd been right, there was no way it was going to get out.

She killed the engine, pocketed the keys, and started to walk down the road.

Georgia realized that she wasn't that far away from the women she'd passed, the women she'd stolen the car from.

She walked for less than a minute, when she realized that her ankle must have been twisted.

She tried to push on, simply gritting her teeth and continuing, but the pain was completely overwhelming. Each step she took was pure agony.

She looked behind her. There was no sign of the three women. And what motivation did they have to follow her? They couldn't have thought they would have any chance of catching up to her on foot.

But then again, there was the possibility that they'd heard the crash and would come to investigate.

The rain was pouring down.

For the first time, Georgia heard the tremendous crack of thunder far away in the sky.

It startled her. She was soaking wet, already drenched to the bone, and shivering.

She sat down on the side of the road to consider her options. There was no way she was going to make it back on this ankle alone.

But she was resourceful, and she wasn't going to give up just yet, especially when the safety of her kids was at stake.

So she found a small sapling, fished out her pocket knife, and set to work cutting it down as best she could. She made the cuts at an angle, and used the non-serrated blade to make sawing motions. She bent the sapling down from the top, using the pressure to increase the effectiveness of her cuts. She didn't know much about bushcrafting, but she must have understood some of the basics, because it worked.

In less than ten minutes, she was back on the road, using the cut sapling as a rudimentary crutch.

She gritted her teeth through the pain and used the crutch to help her damaged ankle. She still had to put some weight on it, but it was better than before. Soon the crutch was digging horribly into her armpit, but she did the best she could. She stopped in the pouring rain and picked up some soaking wet dead leaves on the side of the road. She stuffed them into the crook of her armpit to use as padding against the end of the sapling.

But it was still hurting. So she stopped yet again, took off her soaking wet shirt. She balled that up, then stuffed the leaves inside the shirt. It made a much better pad for the crutch, and she was able to walk at a slow yet purposefull pace down the road.

She was freezing, wearing just her bra. But the shirt wouldn't have helped much anyway.

Georgia hadn't seen rain this intense in a long, long time. She could barely see more than twenty yards in front of her.

The thunder was getting closer, and she saw lightning in the distance. The storm was upon her.

As she moved, her large breasts bobbled in front of her. The bra was soaked and had become uncomfortable when wet. The straps dug into her skin. She considered taking off the bra, but her breasts had always been uncomfortably big without a bra when doing any physical activity.

There was a sound behind her. It was hard, if not impossible, to tell what it was, because of the noise of the growing storm, the cracks of thunder, and the pounding rain.

But there it was. She heard it now. It was a scream. A human screaming, cutting through the rain.

Georgia stopped and turned around, supporting herself as best she could on the crutch.

She felt vulnerable for the first time in a long time. Maybe it wasn't wearing a shirt, having her breasts exposed in the soaking bra, having the crutch, being impossibly fatigued and hungry. Whatever it was, it was a new feeling for her, and she didn't like it. She didn't feel ready to confront whoever it was that was coming.

Her mind turned to the women whose car she'd taken. It must have been them.

She felt guilty and stupid. She'd stolen their car and gotten it stuck. What had been the point of all this? She felt like a failure. But she wasn't just going to sit in the woods and wait to die. She was going to do what she had to do to get back to her kids. If that meant fighting off these women, then that would be what she had to do.

"Hey! Yeah, you!"

Georgia still couldn't see the women through the thick rain. Not yet. They must have been right out of her sight.

Georgia took the crutch from the ground and held it like a club. She was ready to defend herself.

She was wobbly on her legs, her ankle about to give out.

She was so tired it wasn't until she finally saw the woman approaching that she remembered she had two guns with her.

But was she ready to use it? Ready to defend herself against someone who she'd wronged?

The three woman appeared before her. They were soaking in the rain. Their faces were contorted in pure anger. They were ready. For what, Georgia didn't know.

20

MAX

The rain was falling heavily, and Max could hear thunder in the distance. The ground was already turning to a thick mud, and Max was glad that he'd changed into boots earlier.

His stomach was empty and his wrist was killing him. He was looking forward to getting back in the Jeep, driving to a safe, secluded spot, and finally setting up the camping stove. They still had a ton of perishable food taken from his refrigerator as well as Mandy's. The stuff from the refrigerator was not chilled, but some of it might still be good. He'd be willing to eat just about anything now.

He knew that he'd taken a couple pounds of frozen chicken.

Despite his misgivings about the situation, Max realized that in a way Mandy was right.

These guys and the people in the town were in the same situation that Max and Mandy were.

They passed by the Jeep.

"I just want to check on Chad," said Max. Really, he wanted to make sure that everything was there.

He did a once over on the Jeep. The keys were still in it. And everything inside seemed to still be there.

Chad was lying on his back in the mud next to the Jeep. The rain was falling heavily on him, and he was already soaked.

"How you doing, Chad?" said Max. "Those guys hurt you bad?"

"Nah, man," said Chad. His voice had a dreamy, happy quality to it. "I'm good, man. I'm good."

"You got your pills, then?" said Max, not bothering to hide the disgust in his voice.

"Yeah, man, I'm all right."

Max left him there lying in the mud. Chad didn't seem to care that he was wet and muddy.

Max wondered briefly why he'd bothered rescuing Chad. Maybe he'd have been better off getting beaten to death by that mob. That was a horrible thought, but that was what it was.

Max joined Mandy and the men. They introduced themselves to each other, shaking hands.

It was a little awkward at first, considering what had happened.

Mandy and Max told them about the men Max had knocked out in the back of the store. The men had just laughed it off, and gone to check to see if he was OK.

That guy's name was Jim, and he joined them.

Once his buddies explained to him that Max and Mandy definitely weren't foreign spies, he warmed up to them a little more, and he warmed up to them even further when he heard that they were going to check on Tod's sick dad.

Tod's house was up a little side street. The six of them trudged through the rain together, chatting idly.

Max was tired and exhausted and he knew that Mandy

was too. The men, however, were much better fed. They'd been up all night, but they'd been eating hot dogs.

When Max asked them about it, it turned out the majority of them had large basements full of canned and nonperishable foods. They might not have been outright preppers, but they definitely were in that general area.

Tod's house was cluttered, and it was clear that he didn't have much money.

His wife and his two kids were introduced. They seemed like a sweet family.

Max pondered on how strange it was that an hour ago, they'd all been convinced the other party were dangerous enemies. Now, Max and Mandy were invited into the house, shaking hands with Tod's wife, saying hi to the kids.

Tod's wife had set out candles, which made the place seem not as creepy as it otherwise would have been, without power, the rain pounding down on the roof.

"Yup," said one of the men. Max couldn't remember his name. Names had never been his strong suit. "Looks like a storm's really starting outside."

It was true. Max could feel it in his bones. He was feeling worried about moving on out, but he had the idea that maybe he, Mandy, and Chad would be invited to stay here for the night, and continue on the next morning.

"Where's your dad?" said Mandy.

"He's upstairs."

Tod led them upstairs. It was just Tod, Mandy, and Max. The rest stayed downstairs, huddled around the warmth of the fire.

Max wished he was downstairs too, drying out. He wished he could eat, and fall asleep by the fire, and never have to worry again about the difficult journey ahead of them.

It hadn't been that long since the EMP, but already he was fatigued beyond the point he would have thought possible.

What was more, he didn't know why they were going to see this sick man. It wasn't like Max was a doctor. He'd worked in an office, and medical care and first aid were weak points of his.

"Were you ever a nurse or something?" whispered Max to Mandy, as he followed her up the stairs.

She shook her head. "I thought maybe we could help."

Max sighed. He just didn't see how they were going to help.

He couldn't help checking out Mandy's ass as he followed her up the stairs. Even wearing pants, her legs looked long, shapely, and athletic, and her ass was muscular, firm, yet just large enough. And her pants being soaked didn't help keep Max's attention away. His eyes felt drawn to it like a magnet.

"Pop," said Tod, already entering his father's room. "There are some people here to see you. They wanted to see how you're doing... We thought they were foreign spies, but it turns out they're just from Pennsylvania like us."

"Aw, shucks," said Max, walking into the room. "Yeah, turns out we weren't spies at all..."

Tod gave Max a confused look. Max supposed he himself was still a little bitter about the whole being imprisoned experience. And he also supposed that Tod wasn't really up on sarcasm, or irony, or whatever it was Max was employing.

"How are you doing, sir?" said Mandy, kneeling down by the man.

He was propped up in his chair, various pillows helping to support him.

Max studied him. He looked like he was dying all right. Max knew that dialysis was serious business. Without it, this man would die, and there wasn't anything he or Mandy could do about it.

Max knew that Mandy must have already known that. But she was a deeply caring person in a lot of ways. She wanted to confront the suffering of others head on. She didn't want to run away from it.

Max wasn't sure whether he wanted to run away from it or not.

The man looked really sick. Max hadn't seen someone in this bad of shape for a long, long time. He had a slightly blueish tint to his skin, and he was breathing laboriously.

"How's it going, sir?" said Mandy again.

"She asked how you're doing, Pop," said Tod.

The man looked at Tod and then at Mandy. His eyes went down to her breasts, and he stared at them for a moment.

"Good to see some nice sights around here," he said.

"Don't listen to him," said Tod, blushing in embarrassment for what his father had said.

"It's fine," said Mandy. "How are you feeling, sir?"

"Pain," said the man, his face going blank. "Pain, nothing but pain."

Mandy looked at Max, who shrugged his shoulders ever so slightly. He didn't see why they were here, except that Mandy had too big of a heart.

"Come on, Mandy," he said. "We should be getting out of here." There went his dreams of sleeping by the fire and having a good meal before getting back on the seemingly never ending road, filled with rain and storms, and countless obstacles that he still had yet to cross.

"Pain," said the man. "I knew it would end soon. I had a

feeling about this. When the power went out, I shrugged it off. But then my kids were telling me their phones weren't working. I'm headed out, and that's fine. I had a good run, I just didn't know the end would seem so bleak and... painful. I just..."

He slumped a little in his chair, tired with the fatigue of having to speak for so long.

"What are you giving him for the pain?" said Mandy.

Max didn't know what kind of pain the guy would be in. Max associated pain with broken wrists, broken bones, blunt trauma, that sort of thing. Maybe back pain, too, not that he'd ever had much of an issue with that.

"Just some aspirin," grunted Tod. "We don't have much more than that."

"Well, what about those pills Chad has?" she said to Max.

"I'll go get them," said Max instantly.

Chad didn't need those damn pills. But this guy did.

"I'll be right back," said Max, nodding to Tod, who nodded back.

Max jogged down the stairs despite his growing fatigue. His wrist was still killing him.

The rain outside was heavy, but Max was already wet. The thunder was crashing all around. It sounded like a bowling alley on steroids. Lightning flickered in the sky. The wind was intense. The trees swayed in the gusts like they would fall over.

The town looked different in the rain and the storm. It looked like a little oasis, a little haven being battered by the forces of nature.

Max knew that his own journey was changing. That was what the storm meant to him. So far, he'd escaped the clutches of his dying civilization. He'd battled other humans. He'd shot two of them. He'd done what he had to do to get out.

The further out he got, the less people he would encounter. That was going to be the big change for Max, and whoever was going to come with him.

Max knew what the future held. It was this storm. This storm was it.

Max would be facing nature, wild and intense, dangerous and possibly disastrous. There wasn't any way to prepare for that. Sure, he had some gear. He had the Jeep. He had the guns.

But it would be him against not just the elements, but against the faceless void that people called mother nature, the unsympathetic beast composed of a thousand beasts all together.

There would be moments, Max knew, when he would be hungry and cold. He would be on the verge of starvation, unless he could use his own wits to outpace what was going to come for him no matter what. That was death, cold and silent, the grim reaper facing him down with a pointed scythe and not a care in the world, breathless and boney.

Max knew there was no end in sight. Civilization had collapsed. Gone were the comfy baths, gone was hot water entirely. Gone was everything he'd known. Gone was the fast food. Gone were the grocery stories and the automobiles. Once the gas was finished, there would be no more point to the Jeep. There'd be no point to his cook stove either.

Max would have to learn everything again. He'd have to do what people had done on this planet for hundreds of thousands of years, and that was survive, even when the faceless void yawned its impressive toothless grin right in his pitiful human face.

But there was hope. There was a way to cheat death. And that wasn't mere survival. It wasn't finding comfort among the wilderness. It was procreation—creating more humans so that the human race could continue. For how long, no one knew. An eternity stretched in front of him, a great chasm from which there was no return, and year by year it would swallow the humans given to it. It would swallow them eagerly without compulsion or feeling. The human race would continue mating, giving birth, dying, throwing humans right into that ceaseless void, wherever it was, wherever it appeared. It would swallow that old man up soon enough, and it would swallow Max up when it had the chance.

Max must have been more tired than he'd thought. This was heavy shit he was thinking about. His mind seemed to be reeling. It seemed to be in some strange place.

The rain pounding forcefully onto him, Max approached the Jeep.

"Chad!" he screamed. "Get up! What the hell are you doing?"

Chad was lying in a pool of muddy water, the rain pounding down onto him.

He was facing the ceaseless void of nature, the intense majestic forces that could destroy him in an instant without a care.

They were up against nature. And it wasn't just Max and Chad. It was everyone, everywhere.

Chad had never looked happier. A huge grin was plastered on his face.

"Chad!" screamed Max, bending down and putting his mouth right to his ear.

"Huh?" said Chad, finally realizing that Max was there. He was as high as a kite.

"Get up, Chad," said Max.

He bent down and picked up the immensely heavy Chad. He seemed heavier now than he had before, if that was even possible. It was just the illusion the water was providing. Heavier things were always wet, and Chad was one of them.

"Hey, man," said Chad, his eyes glossy and his pupils wide. "Funny seeing you here."

"You think I could have one of those pills, man?" said Max. He knew that if talked Chad's language, he'd hand then over.

"Sure, man," said Chad. "I'm happy you've finally come around. You were always such a square, man. But now that civilization's ending, you're coming around... I like that, man."

He handed the pills to Max. Max checked them. Fortunately, no water was getting into the airtight bottle.

Max shook the pills, hearing the sound of them rattling around.

"You know, there aren't going to be any more of these," said Max. "There aren't any more factories to make them. You know that, right?"

"I know, man," said Chad. "But got to enjoy it while you can, right?"

"Sure, man," said Max, talking down to him, but Chad didn't even notice. "Got to enjoy it while you can. But you realize you're going to have to face the withdrawal sooner or later, right?"

"Sure, man," said Chad, a happy look on his face. He wasn't all there. "Say, aren't you going to take one of those pills?"

"Yeah," said Max. "I'm going to take all of them."

"I tried that once," said Chad vaguely. "Ended up in the hospital."

"I'm giving them all to a dying guy," said Max. "He actually needs them."

"What?" said Chad, despair suddenly appearing on his face and in his voice. "You can't do that! They're mine."

"I can do what I want," said Max. "I saved you. The only reason you're alive is because of me... because of our past. And you know what? You're completely useless. And this guy needs the pills way more than you. He actually needs them. You? You're just a coward."

Max started walking swiftly away. He pulled his jacket close to him, to keep the gales of wind from blowing it open.

Chad ran after him. Max could hear his footsteps splashing in puddles.

"Give me the pills," he shouted.

Max didn't answer.

He didn't even turn around.

The next thing he knew, Chad's fist hit him in side of the face. It was a hard blow, and Max reeled from it, almost losing his balance.

"You don't want to fight me," said Max. It took every ounce of his self-control not to hit Chad back. But he knew that it would just create more problems for him later on. If he seriously injured Chad, he'd be the one who had to deal with it. That was his code of honor, his own system by which he had to live by, even if no one else did.

Chad growled like an animal. "Give me those pills," he said. There was spittle coming out of his mouth. His face was flushed and red. He seemed not to notice the wind or the rain in the slightest.

Chad charged at him, lowering himself as if he was going to tackle Max.

Max stepped to the side easily and stuck out his leg. Chad tripped over it, and went flying face first into the mud.

Max was disgusted by his behavior, and didn't even turn around to look at him, to see how he was.

He opened the door again, fighting the wind.

He climbed the stairs with heavy, wet footsteps.

"Here you go," he said, handing the pills to Tod.

"He should take one whenever he feels discomfort," said Mandy, who looked like she'd dried off just a little bit.

"What are you, a nurse?" said Max.

She didn't answer.

The old dying man was asleep now, but Max could see the pain still on his face. He was glad that he would have the pills, and not Chad, but he knew that now he'd have to deal with Chad in withdrawal mania for however long it took for that shit to leave his system completely.

Max wanted to do nothing more than collapse on the floor downstairs, by the fire.

But he knew that wasn't happening. Not that Tod wasn't grateful. In fact, he wouldn't shut up about it. He was saying that these pills would give his dad some relief in his final moments.

Max was beyond exhausted. He kept repeating to himself that he was exhausted, like a tape-recorded voice that wouldn't stop in his head.

The world around him seemed to be fading. His mind was over-active. People's voices were getting dimmer, and less important.

But one thing he could read loud and clear was the expression on Mandy's face.

He saw it on her as clear as day. He saw how empathetic she was, how much it pained her to see this man dying, to consider all the people around the world in pain, dying without assistance, dying from starvation and a thousand horrors.

"Come on, Mandy," said Max.

He took her hand and it felt warm in his. His own felt cold and clammy.

They said goodbye, and declined all offers of a hot meal from the fire. Max knew they had to be moving on. The faster they got to their destination, the better.

They walked hand in hand into the storm, into the rain, into the chaos of the natural world.

"What's going to happen to everyone?" said Mandy. Her voice sounded distant.

Max didn't answer.

He knew what she meant.

He was wondering the same thing. Somehow he'd been able to hold it all back until now, the thoughts of what this really meant.

He'd been so focused on his own personal survival, on what he needed to do to get out. In a way, that was a defense strategy, a personal thought shield against the true horrors of considering humanity at large right now.

If the entire world had experienced the EMP, which Max was thinking was more and more likely, given the complete lack of communication or help from the outside, then... well, everything was screwed.

He didn't know how else to put it to himself. Images of children, men, women, elderly... all over the world... dying a thousand deaths. He felt like the Buddha, under that tree right after enlightenment, when he confronted the suffering of the world. There was no great force to confront, no greater pain to battle...

"Are you OK, Max?" said Mandy.

"Huh?" said Max.

"You have that faraway look in your eyes. Are you OK?"

"My wrist is fine," said Max.

"I meant... you know, how are you feeling?"

"I'm fine," said Max. "But you better drive. My wrist is still messed up."

"I thought it was fine?"

Max didn't answer her.

"Chad!" yelled Max.

Chad was knocked out cold in the mud.

"What happened to him?"

"Who knows," said Max. "Now help me get him into the Jeep."

They dragged him towards the Jeep, not taking too much care with his body.

"What's your deal with this guy, anyway?" said Mandy.

"Long story," said Max.

21

J ames and Sadie drove through the storm. Unlike the pickup, which rattled and shook with the slightest bump, the SUV was brand new. And that meant that it felt completely insulated from the outside world.

The radio and CD player didn't work, and there was no tape deck. But aside from the lack of music, it felt like they were back in civilization, just by sitting in the comfort of the SUV.

"I wish the seat warmers worked," said Sadie.

"Shut up," said James. "And help me look for Mom, won't you?"

"What do you think I'm doing?"

"Wait," said James, trying his best to peer through the rain. The windshield whipers were going as fast as they could. "I think that's her!"

"But who are those other people?"

James stopped the car near his mother and three other figures. It was hard to see what was going on in the rain.

"You stay here," said James, getting out of the car.

"Wait, what do I do?" said Sadie, but James closed the door before he heard what she was saying.

"Mom!" shouted James, over the tremendous noise of the storm. "Are you OK?"

His mother didn't have her shirt on. She was soaked to the bone. She had some kind of crutch under her arm.

"James!" she shouted, hobbling over to him as fast as she could.

She hugged him.

"Are you OK?" she said, upon seeing the SUV.

James explained briefly what had happened, without really touching on what had happened to the driver of the SUV.

"But the driver?" said Georgia.

James just shook his head and didn't answer her.

"Oh," she said.

"Who are they?" said James, gesturing to the people he now recognized as middle-aged women.

"Oh," said Georgia. "It's a long story... We've just been chatting out here in the rain."

"Chatting?"

"Yeah," said Georgia. "It was the funniest thing. You see, it was their car I stole..."

His mother seemed tired, but she seemed with it. In fact, she seemed in better spirits than he'd seen her in a while.

"Truthfully, it's been great. I don't get to hang out with women my own age that much. They're the funniest girls you'll ever meet. Girls, get over here."

It was a little surreal for James to be introduced to three of his mother's new friends out here in the middle of the storm, in the midst of the collapse of civilization.

Georgia called Sadie out of the car, and then Sadie was introduced to them too.

James had trouble remember their names, at first, but in the end he learned that they were named Shirley, Bobby-Jean, and Norma.

They were old fashioned names, but maybe around these parts they were normal. James wasn't sure.

They talked for what seemed like forever. Georgia and her new friends didn't seem to mind the rain. Occasionally James wondered about their sanity—had they snapped, or been hit in the head?

But then he realized what had happened—it was just one of those strange reactions to stress that you hear about sometimes, when people act the opposite of how you would expect them to react.

After what seemed like forever, Georgia finally suggested that they go see about the car that she'd crashed.

"Looks like it's going to be a while before we get some rest," said James, climbing back into the SUV.

"Oh, this is a nice car," said Shirley, or Norma, or whoever it was.

"This is fun," said Bobby-Jean.

Georgia and the women chatted all the way to the car.

"Looks like you really did a number on that one," said James. "I'll see if I can get it out."

While Sadie, his mother, and the other women waited in the comfort of the plush SUV, James battled the rain and the storm. He found some chains that he'd taken from the pickup and set about attaching them.

James didn't know a ton about cars. There was a hitch on the SUV, of course, but at first there didn't seem to be anything on the compact car. In the end, he figured out that he could punch a hole through some superficial decorative metal on the rear end, and wrap the chain around the bumper through the hole. He figured now that society was collapsing, no one would care about a little cosmetic damage to the car.

"Here goes nothing," said James, getting back into the car, starting it up. He shifted it into reverse, and slowly pressed the accelerator.

"How fun!" said Norma.

"Are you insane or something?" said James.

Norma just laughed.

His mother laughed along with her.

"We're not crazy," said Georgia. "Not yet, anyway. We're just trying to make the best of this situation. Would you believe I pointed my gun at these lovely women?"

They all had a good laugh over that. Meanwhile, James concentrated on pulling the car off the side of the road, while trying not to run off the road himself.

It wouldn't have made any difference if someone had been outside, since the rain was so thick James wouldn't have been able to see anything.

Meanwhile, night was falling. Another pitch black night. This time, accompanied by a storm.

Finally, after what seemed like forever, the car was free.

James got out and tested the car to see if it was drivable, while the three ladies watched.

"I think you'll be fine," he said. "Looks OK. Uh, sorry my mom crashed it."

"Don't worry about it, dear," said one of the women. "We won't be using it much anyway. We just thought it would be fun to have it."

"Fun to have it?"

"You know, for pleasure drives."

James didn't know what to say. The more he talked to these women, the crazier he thought they were. They didn't seem like they were attached to reality at all. They certainly wouldn't last much longer. Who knew what kind of people would come along, bad people, once the cities started spilling their chaos into these parts.

"Oh," said James finally.

"Well, Georgia," said the girls, seeming to speak together. "We're going to get going now. It was so nice to meet you."

There was a lot of hugging and laughing as they women descended from the SUV to get into their little compact car, to drive back to the house they lived in.

"What the hell was that all about?" said Sadie, speaking for the first time in a while.

"They're just..."

Georgia suddenly seemed tragically sad.

"Mom, what's going on?" said James. "What was that all about? You stole their car, crashed it, and suddenly you're best friends with them?"

"Let's just drive, James," said Georgia, sniffling a little bit.

"Mom, are you crying?" said Sadie.

"Just drive," said Georgia.

James had never seen his mother like this. She was hardened, normally. She could take anything. She didn't just start crying.

James drove on, down the rain drenched road. The SUV handled the curves beautifully. The tires seemed to stick right to the road.

Sadie fell asleep quickly. She was simply too exhausted.

James would have liked to take a nap, but he had to drive. He had a job to do. And that, in a way, made him feel good.

"Mom," he said quietly, so as not to wake Sadie. "What was all that about?"

"James," said Georgia. "I'm just starting to realize how

terrible this all is. This situation. I mean, can you imagine what everyone all over is going through? People realize that society is going to break down, or already has broken down... People aren't prepared. The world is going to turn into a terrible, terrible place. Just because we're going to be far away from it all, doesn't mean it isn't going to happen."

"I know, Mom," said James.

"Those women," said Georgia, "are incredibly sweet. And they're intelligent. They're roommates, and best friends. They realize that they're not prepared, and they fully understand what's happening. Well, as fully as anyone can understand what's happening to us."

"I don't get it," said James. "If they're not prepared, and they know what's going on, then why were they so happy? Why were you laughing with them?"

"They have a somewhat... unique philosophy. They want to live life to the fullest, to have as much fun as possible."

"I don't get it."

"When they no longer have enough food," said Georgia. "They're going to commit suicide. They have the pills already and everything."

"Oh," said James. He remained quiet for some time.

"James," said Georgia. "I want you to know that that's not an option for anyone in our family. That's simply not going to happen. We're going to make it. We're not like everyone else. We're going to make it, James."

"I know," said James. "I know."

But the gravity of the situation, the perils ahead, suddenly struck him harder than they ever had before.

James kept driving the shiny new SUV into the darkening rain-drenched night. The thunder was all around them. James could barely see fifteen feet in front of them, but he kept driving. He had to. He had to save them.

22

CHAD

Chad couldn't believe it. He woke up, drenched in sweat. But he was freezing cold.

His head ached like nothing he'd ever felt before.

He couldn't remember what had happened for a full minute, and he stayed silent, in the hopes that people around him would talk.

He then realized he didn't know where he was, or who he was with.

Was he with Marty and Danny again, on some kind of crazy mission, some midnight mischief?

He was in a car, in the backseat. He knew that much. They were driving through a horrible storm, somewhere way out in the woods.

Chad tried to stay silent, but it was too much for him.

"Danny, where the hell are you taking us, man? And what happened to my head?"

"Danny? Who the hell are you talking about?"

It all came gushing back to Chad. The memories.

The end of civilization. Oh yeah.

Damn it.

And then he remembered the worst part: he didn't have his pills.

Max had stolen them from him, and then knocked him out.

Chad knew that he was going through withdrawal, which was strange, since one of the last things he remembered was being high off his ass. So that meant he must have been knocked out for a long, long time. No wonder his head ached so much.

"You gave my pills away, didn't you?" he said to Max.

"Yeah, Chad," said Max. "I did."

"It was for a good cause, Chad," said Mandy, speaking kindly. "There was a dying man. He was in so much pain... And you're going to have to go through withdrawal anyway."

On some level, Chad knew that he just wanted to be a dick because of withdrawal. He knew that it was screwing with his emotions. With everything. He knew that he wasn't himself, but then again, he didn't really know who he actually was. He didn't know *where* he himself was.

Chad took a deep breath to try to calm himself.

But the rage was already pouring through him. It was too late.

"Shut the hell up, you sexy little bitch," said Chad. "What the hell do you know about what I've been through?"

"Hey!" yelled Max. "Don't talk to her like that, Chad. She doesn't deserve that. I'm the one who gave the pills away."

"You asshole," said Chad. "Stop the car. I'm getting out. I don't need your shit."

"Where you going to go, buddy?" said Max. "You're going to wander around the woods until you starve to death, or until someone finds you and decides you're starting to look juicy to their grumbling stomach. You want to die, or be killed and eaten? Tortured? What do you want to happen, Chad?"

"I don't give a damn," said Chad.

He tried to open the door, but it didn't open.

"Why won't this piece of shit open?"

"I've got the child safety lock on," said Max.

"You sanctimonious piece of shit," shouted Chad. "Let me go die in peace."

"Screw you, Chad," said Max.

"Screw you, too."

Chad lunged forward, not caring what happened to himself. He just wanted to express his rage. He wanted to hurt Max. He didn't care that Max had saved him.

It happened too fast for Chad to understand what was happening.

Mandy swung something at him, something hard and made of metal. It collided with his skull, and he fell instantly unconscious yet again.

23

NORMA

The world was ending.

Norma had moved out here with her two best friends after college. It was supposed to be just for a summer, but it was a summer that had never ended. They were all very close, and shared everything together, gossip about the men they were dating, their wine, their clothes.

They'd all gotten jobs and stayed through the first season. Now it was over twenty years later, and the world was ending.

Norma hadn't thought that it would end this way.

Her parents had died. Her brothers and sisters had moved far away a long time ago.

Norma had enjoyed the area, going for hikes and walks, learning to fish. She'd taught middle school there, and her two roommates had worked as clerks at a grocery store. None of them needed much money—they split the rent, and didn't exactly spend a lot. They'd all shared the one compact car.

It was an unusual lifestyle, but it had worked for the three of them. They'd all gone to school in New York City.

That was back when the city was a real hell hole, and they all wanted to get out, get back to nature, that sort of thing.

That was the time when all the hippies were dropping out of society. They were moving to California, down south, out west, abroad, Canada, wherever they thought they could start over. Norma had never been a hippie, but something about the movement had been appealing.

Things hadn't seemed right when the power went off. The phones didn't work. People from the nearby town were driving by, acting all crazy. People were freaking out.

A couple military vehicles had driven by, types that she'd never seen before. The soldiers warned her that the United States was under attack. They said the roads were all closed to the city, and to the nearby areas.

It didn't seem like the US was under attack. But something was definitely wrong. Very wrong.

There was no way to get food.

Norma's encounter with Georgia had solidified this in her mind. She knew there was no way she and her friends would live.

But Norma couldn't bring them along with her, for where she was about to go.

Norma had struggled with depression for years. Sure, she'd had fun. But the depression always came back, that black hole that seemed to swallow her up.

The woods were nice, despite the rain.

The storm seemed beautiful, in a way. It was nature at work, in full force. Nature would swallow up the planet. Life would go on. Maybe not so much human life. But there would be survivors, and eventually things would get back to where they were. Maybe the survivors would warn their descendants about what had happened, and some mistakes could be avoided.

But Norma didn't have a lot of confidence that things would improve. She knew that humans had set things up horribly, practically destroyed the planet in doing so. Maybe they deserved what was coming to them. Norma didn't know.

The black hole of depression was there. But it was easing up.

They'd asked if Norma was OK, if she was sure she wanted to go walking alone during the storm.

She'd told them she was fine, that she'd always loved the rain.

They'd been worried, but they were tired, and didn't want to argue with her. They understood that sometimes she needed to be alone, even if it seemed crazy, even if there was a storm outside.

The wind was crashing into her. The lightning was flashing in the sky.

If only the lighting would hit her, and just take her out...

But she couldn't rely on that.

The pain pills were in her pocket, a whole bottle of them. She'd gotten them when she'd sprained her ankle years ago, but she'd always been scared of medication, and had never taken a single one of the pills.

Norma knew that taking the whole bottle would kill her. There was no doubt about that. She would simply slip away, fade away. It wasn't like anyone would find her, here, deep in the forest.

There was no chance of being rescued, and that was the way she wanted it.

She took the bottle out and rattled them. As she opened it up, the pills started to get wet. But that wouldn't hurt them.

She swallowed them one by one, taking sips from the plastic water bottle she carried everywhere.

After the tenth one, she was already feeling strange. Sleepy. Hard to describe... Her thoughts were a little fuzzy. Disjointed. A little odd...

Norma powered through, taking the pills one by one, diligently. She was taking her medicine. The pills would make everything go away. They would make everything better...

Norma didn't believe in heaven. But she knew that she just didn't want to exist anymore.

She thought of her family, of her friends. She thought of the opportunities she'd never taken. But she'd had a good life. In a way.

She thought of her depression, that depression that had haunted her even when things were going well, that dark yawning chasm that screamed her name in the night, that kept her awake and kept her heart pounding.

That chasm would disappear completely. She would never feel that pain again.

Norma was soaked to the bone. She sat down in the mud, no longer caring. The pill bottle dropped out of her limp hand.

She was still conscious, but it was fading.

She no longer was aware of the storm, of the intensity of the natural world around her.

She was no longer aware that she was in the mud. If she had been, she wouldn't have cared.

Norma was high for the first time in her life, as high as she ever would be. Her body felt light and free. Her mind felt suddenly unencumbered by all the things she'd worried about.

Norma tried to move her hand, but nothing happened. She was losing control of her body.

Slowly, her breathing changed. It slowed to a snail's pace. Her breaths were miniscule, barely noticeable.

Her mind was somewhere else, floating away, up through the sunshine that wasn't there, up through a cloudless sky that had never existed.

Norma didn't want to have to fight. She didn't want to struggle. She didn't want to survive.

She got what she wanted.

24

MAX

"Are you sure we're going the right way?" said Mandy.

"No," said Max. "But I don't know what else to do. There aren't any other roads here."

"Maybe we should turn around," said Mandy, peering down at the maps. Her flashlight had already died, so she was using Max's, ignoring his pleas for her to conserve the battery as much as possible. "I don't know. I just don't have any idea where we are."

"It's hard to tell in this storm," said Max.

The high beams of the Jeep were barely cutting through the night. The Jeep was wracked by the wind, shifting from side to side constantly. The rain pounded onto the roof and the windows, making so much noise they had to almost shout to be heard by each other.

"How do you think he's doing?" said Mandy, looking back at Chad, who was passed out in the backseat.

"He's fine," said Max gruffly.

"I hit him pretty hard," said Mandy. "I hope I didn't hurt him too badly."

"He deserved it," said Max.

"Are you sure we shouldn't turn around?"

Max didn't answer. He kept driving. He was hungry and tired and his wrist was killing him.

Tensions were rising between Max and Mandy. Max had insisted that they keep driving all night, and then they could rest in the morning.

Mandy, on the other hand, had wanted to hole up in the Jeep and wait out the storm.

Max was feeling a constant urge, a constant pressure to push forward. He was done with being extremely cautious. They had run into too many problems already. In his mind, the sooner they got to the farm house, the better. There, they could relax, they could eat. They could rest up and plan for what was coming next.

Max didn't know how long it would be before more people arrived from the city, provided they were able to get out at all. But he didn't want to wait around to find out. He didn't want to be traveling the open road when they came. He wanted to be safely at the farm house.

He already had plans for some rudimentary defenses that he was going to set up. A ditch surrounding the property, for instance, would slow down intruders. And once he ran out of gas for the Jeep, he might be able to use the car battery to create an electric fence. He didn't know if there would be enough power or how long it would last for, though.

Unless the farm house had been raided, there was food there, and guns. But as far as Max knew, no one had been to the property in a few years. Who knew what had happened to it in that time. He didn't have any idea what kind of condition it would be in, whether it would be boarded up. Would the water work after an EMP? Max simply didn't know.

Max had wanted to save time, to push on through the storm. But even he had to admit that they were probably headed the wrong way. They might be headed farther away from the farmhouse now. He had no idea. But he was stuck somewhere in his own stubbornness, and his foot kept pressing the accelerator pedal.

"Look!" said Mandy. "Lights!"

Max peered through the windshield. He could barely make out some lights ahead.

"Headlights, you think?" said Max.

"I don't know," muttered Mandy.

He couldn't see the road, and he didn't know whether the lights were coming from the road or off the road.

He was so tired his brain didn't seem to be working correctly. Lights... he was thinking. That's kind of strange. Isn't all the power out? He knew he was missing something, but he wasn't sure what it was.

"They must be headlights," said Mandy. "Should you pull over? We don't want to run into them."

Max grunted a negative.

He didn't want to get off the road now. The sides of the road had become flooded mud ditches, from which the Jeep might never return if it entered there.

The lights got closer.

"They're definitely headlights," said Mandy.

"I think you're right," said Max. "They're still really far off..."

"Wait," said Mandy. "What happened? They're gone."

Sure enough, the headlights were completely gone now.

"Did they turn them off?" said Max.

"Shit," said Mandy. "We'll never see them if they have their headlights off..."

Max slowed down as he drove forward, doing his best to keep his eyes glued to where the phantom car might appear.

Turning their headlights off was a bad sign in Max's mind. The car had been far off, but it must have seen their own lights. If they were good people, Max couldn't imagine them turning off their headlights, However, if they were bad guys, maybe they'd turn their headlights off in an attempt to ambush Max and Mandy.

Max drove on. Ten minutes passed.

There was no sign of the oncoming car.

"That was really weird," said Mandy, in a hushed and worried voice. "What do you think happened to them?"

"No idea," said Max. "We just need to keep going. It's better to get out of here, especially if there's another car in the area. We don't know anything about them or what they want."

"That's your solution to everything," said Mandy. "You just want to keep going and going, even if we don't know where we're headed."

Suddenly, the Jeep was filled with bright, powerful light.

It was the headlights again, but they were coming at them from the side.

It was too late. Max realized at the last second what had happened. Without realizing it, they had driven right through a crossroads.

The other car, with its high beams still on, was coming at them from the side.

The other car T-boned them.

There was the horrible sound of the collision. The sound of metal crunching. The sound of screams.

The other vehicle hit the Jeep's engine, pushing it sideways in a horrible jerking motion.

Max was thrown forward. The seatbelt caught him and

jerked him back. His head whiplashed backwards, hurting instantly.

The airbag deployed, but only partially, filling up like some old stock stuffed with quarters

The airbag didn't even touch Max.

He didn't lose consciousness. He looked over at Mandy. There wasn't an airbag on her side. But the seatbelt had saved her. She hadn't lost consciousness, but she looked dazed.

A thousand thoughts ran through Max's head at once. The Jeep. The damn Jeep. It was no doubt ruined. Without it, things were going to be a *lot* tougher.

But Max knew that the Jeep was a more long-term worry. The immediate, short term worry was who'd crashed into them and why.

Max cut his seatbelt with a pocket knife. He tried the release button of Mandy's seatbelt, but it was jammed, so he sliced through that too.

People were shouting in the other car that had collided with them. Max could barely make out the sounds over the heavy rain and the frequent thunder.

Lightning flashed in the sky nearby, illuminating the entire car. But Max wasn't able to see into the other car, except that it was an enormous SUV.

Max didn't have time to evaluate the damage. He moved quickly. He took out his gun, holding it even though his wrist hurt like crazy. He was pretty sure he could hold it well enough to shoot. He'd never practiced using his left hand, and he cursed himself now for that.

He tried his door, but it wouldn't open.

"Out," he whispered to Mandy. "I've got to get out."

"You're going out there?" said Mandy. "Stay in the Jeep, Max."

"I've got to see who they are," said Max. "You can get in the backseat. My door doesn't open. Just let me out."

"If you're going out there, I'm going too," said Mandy.

Max didn't like that. Mandy was unarmed. They'd given the guns back to the village idiots that Mandy had wanted to help. If things had gone Max's way, he would have stolen the guns from them for what they did to them. But that was what compassion would get you.

Despite Max's protests, Mandy got out of the car.

With her door open, the rain was even louder. It made huge crashing sounds as it slammed violently into the pavement.

Mandy was instantly soaked again. Despite the situation, Max's gaze hung for a moment on her soaking chest.

But he tore his eyes away, and clamored over her seat to get out.

He held his flashlight with his left hand, his Glock in his right. He kept the flashlight on the highest setting, knowing that the batteries would drain fast, but he also realized that he hardly had any other choice. No other settings seemed to cut through the night at all.

Max was partially blinded by the raging high beams from the other car. All four headlights (two from each car) were still on, but they had been knocked askew, and they sliced through the night crazily. The headlights and the still-running engines made the night feel chaotic.

Max was instantly wet in the rain.

Lightning slammed into the trees nearby.

Thunder sounded.

Max moved around to the other side of the big black SUV.

He led with his gun, and Mandy stayed behind him. She held the big dead metal flashlight that Max always kept in the Jeep. Presumably, Chad was still passed out. Max hadn't even checked to see if he was OK.

Two doors to the SUV were wide open.

Max pointed his flashlight inside. There was no one there.

There was some gear.

The people couldn't be far...

Max spun around, looking for them, pointing his light through the night.

Suddenly, a powerful light shone on Mandy and Max. It swayed a little, but it stayed right on them.

"Don't move a muscle," came a tough sounding female voice from nearby.

Max froze.

"Don't move," he whispered to Mandy.

"Who are you?" came the voice. It was definitely female, but it had some gravely notes, as if the voice had been toughened and hardened over the years.

Max knew from the voice alone that he was up against a person who wasn't going to take any bullshit. If he was honest with himself, Max was worried.

The last thing he needed right now was to run up against some group of tough women who would steal all their provisions.

"Drop the gun," came the voice.

Max didn't move.

He didn't know what to do. Should he fight? Should he make a stab at shooting her? But there must have been more. Two doors were open, after all. There might be as many as six people out there in the night.

They might all have guns.

Max couldn't even see the woman.

"I'm going to lower it, so there's no chance of an accidental discharge," called out Max, loudly. He had to speak loudly to make his voice heard in the storm.

Max did as he said he would, slowly placing the Glock on the pavement.

"Step away from the gun," came the voice. "Who are you?"

"I'm Max," said Max. He didn't know what to say. It wasn't like he had a serial number or something. And what good would his identity do in a situation like this? Things had changed. Things were different now. His old occupation didn't matter, nor did his driver's license or his library card. His credit cards were worthless, as was his bank account. Now it was just what he had on him. His actions had to speak for themselves.

"How many of you are there?"

Max turned his head a little, trying to see where the light was coming from. It seemed like it was coming from behind some trees off to his left... The people in the SUV must have abandoned their vehicle immediately after the crash. They must not have been injured. Max thought that he'd moved fast, but apparently it hadn't been fast enough.

G eorgia didn't know what to do. She didn't know whether these people were a threat or not.

She wasn't the type to automatically assume that someone was a threat, even in these dire circumstances. But at the same time, the man had rushed out of his car carrying a handgun.

Then again, she had a gun too.

Georgia certainly wasn't just going to murder these people. But she also couldn't just ignore them. They were here, and they weren't simply going to go away. If they were a threat, she'd have to tie them up or something, and that would be the same as murdering them.

Either they were a threat, and she killed them here and now. Or they weren't, and she let them go, let them get their equipment out of their car.

Both vehicles were obviously too damaged to ever run again. It was the sort of damage that totaled the cars. Even a professional mechanic wouldn't be able to help the vehicles.

James was holding the flashlight on them, illuminating

both of them. Sadie was holding a rifle, per Georgia's instructions.

Georgia had to act. She got out from behind the tree and walked towards the man and woman, who had their hands in the air.

Georgia approached them, pointing the gun right at the man's stomach. At this range, there was no chance she could miss. But Georgia also knew about knife attacks. She knew that even trained police officers didn't have time to draw and discharge their weapons if they were rushed with a knife—what was it, something like fifteen feet? It was quite a distance.

So Georgia stayed twenty feet away. She thought that was safe enough, considering the circumstances.

"What are you doing here?" shouted Georgia.

Supposedly the man and women were named Max and Mandy. But they could be lying. Not that it mattered at all.

She studied the man's face, as he squinted in the face of the bright light.

He didn't look dangerous. He looked somewhat serious. But none of that meant anything. Not now.

"We're..."

She could tell the man was hesitating. He didn't want to give away what he was doing.

"Tell me," said Georgia. "Or you're dead."

"We're headed to a house," said the man, supposedly named Max. "This is my friend Mandy... She was my neighbor. We knew we had to get out when the EMP happened. Our friend is in the car. He's knocked out. And he's going through... never mind. He's injured. Not in good condition..."

Georgia had seen the headlights of Max's vehicle earlier. They'd been coming right at them, and Georgia had wanted to avoid them, so she'd taken a turn off to the right.

She realized now what must have happened. It must have just been a small shortcut road that took them right back onto the main road. And when it did, she'd run right into their car, T-boning it.

For the first time in her life, Georgia had absolutely no idea what to do. And she couldn't ask anyone. Her kids were, well, they were just kids. They were teenagers, and they might have thought of themselves as adults, but the truth was that they simply didn't have that adult mindset, the mindset required to make difficult decisions.

Georgia studied the woman's face. She looked kind, in a way. She looked trustworthy, and the man certainly didn't look like any kind of criminal. But all her life Georgia had dealt with people who didn't look like criminals, but had tried to screw her over on her pay, or undercut her in some devious way.

She couldn't stand there forever, in the rain, swaying on her feet from exhaustion.

She went forward, risking it, and grabbed the gun from the man. He didn't move a muscle.

She took the gun, identifying it as a Glock, and stuck it in her waistband carefully.

"Look," said the man. "You've got the upper hand here... You can do what you want. But we're just looking for the same thing you are... We're trying to get out... Trying to survive."

Georgia continued to study him.

The seconds seemed like hours. It felt like an eternity was passing slowly as she kept her gun trained on him.

Finally, the woman spoke.

"We're tired and hungry," she said. "We've been through

so much already. We're not looking to harm anyone. We stopped in a town, and they tied us up and knocked Max out. It turned out they were just scared. They didn't want to hurt us, but they thought we were the enemy, without even knowing us. We ended up helping them, giving them some pain medication for a dying man who couldn't get his dialysis."

She paused.

"Keep going," said Georgia. "I'm listening. Convince me that you're not the enemy, because I don't want you to be. I don't want to have to... hurt you."

"The world is descending into chaos," said the woman named Mandy. "At least as far as we can tell that's happening. Without communication, we don't really know what's happening out there. But before we got out here, we saw a mob descending on a store. They almost killed the man who's passed out in the back of the Jeep. Max saved him, risking both our lives to do so. Society may be collapsing. Society may be dissolving. It's going to be every man and woman against everyone else. Everyone for themselves. But that doesn't mean that we have to act like that. We can help each other. We can share supplies, and... I think we're lost. We need help, too, to be honest."

Georgia made a snap decision. She hoped it wasn't the wrong one.

"Are you hurt?" she said. "From the crash?"

"No," said Max. "We're OK, although we should check on Chad in the back seat."

Georgia lowered her gun. She wasn't sure how much they could see of her.

But they must have been able to see her enough, given the faint diffuse light from the headlights. They instantly relaxed their positions. Max slowly lowered his hands.

Georgia didn't call out for James and Sadie. If something happened to her, she wanted them to be safe. She wanted them to have time to escape. Or for them to shoot and defend themselves.

Georgia walked towards them, her rifle lowered, pointed to the ground.

"I'm Georgia," she said, extending her hand.

She hoped against hope that this wasn't a mistake.

"Max," said Max, shaking her hand.

No funny business. No secret attacks. He just shook her hand and that was it. He had a good, firm grip, and so did Georgia.

She shook Mandy's hand next.

"Where are you two from?"

"Ardmore," said Max.

"Me too," said Mandy. "I'm his next door neighbor. Or was his next door neighbor, I guess."

"I'm from Bryn Mawr," said Georgia.

"Right down the street," said Max, nodding.

"Let's see how your friend is doing, OK?" said Georgia.

The walked around to the other vehicle, a Jeep.

Georgia tried to keep her eyes on Max and Mandy, to make sure they didn't pull anything.

If they proved trustworthy, she would give Max the gun back. But there were so many things that could be weapons. Knives, sticks, flashlights, anything heavy. Georgia didn't see the point of shaking them down, asking for weapons. Plus, she was past that stage. If she was going to do that, she should have done it already.

There was an overweight man passed out in the backseat of the wrecked Jeep.

Max crawled into the back seat to examine him, while

Mandy and Georgia stood somewhat awkwardly outside in the rain, waiting.

Mandy was younger than Georgia, and had a good figure.

"He saved me, you know," said Mandy, making what turned out to be something like small talk. "As soon as the power went out basically, two guys came and tried to... rape me. It was horrible. I didn't even know Max, and he came busting in with his gun drawn and shot them both... They were so horrible. He's always talking about how he has to look out for himself, but he always ends up helping someone. He saved Chad in the back, his old friend. Sorry, I'm kind of rambling on, I guess. I'm just still nervous... The crash really scared me. And we've been through a lot. I'm sure you have too. I don't know what we're going to do now. It looks like the Jeep is totaled."

"Wow," said Georgia. She couldn't think of anything else to say. It was a lot to take in all at once.

"He's OK," said Max, who started to drag his overweight friend out of the car.

He got him down and his friend dropped heavily into the mud.

"He doesn't need to be treated too gently," said Max. "He's an addict... It's a long story, but it's disgusting enough. We gave his pain pills away to someone who actually needed them. Not sure what to do with him."

"What's happening?" said the man.

"We had a car accident, Chad," said Mandy. "Is your head OK?"

Chad lay in the mud. He was already covered in mud from head to toe. He looked completely disgusting. His hair was plastered with mud, long and unruly, covering part of his face. His clothes looked disgusting, like he'd been sweating through them before the rain. They were stained.

"Is he going to be all right?" said Georgia.

"I think so," said Max. "Once he stops being such an asshole. He's been giving us a hard time without his pills. He tried to attack me."

Normally, this would have made Georgia worry for her own safety, but she'd dealt with addicts before. She knew how they behaved, and she knew how horrible it was for them to lose their drug of choice.

"You still with us, Chad?" said Max.

"Still here," muttered Chad. "Not feeling too good though…"

Max got up, leaving Chad in the mud, and started examining the Jeep.

"Looks bad," he said. "I don't think either one of these is going to run again."

"That's what I thought, too," said Georgia. "How far away is the place you're trying to get to?"

"Mandy's been doing the directions," said Max.

"We're lost basically," said Mandy. "At least until day and then maybe things will get clearer. Truth is, I'm so tired now, I can't think straight, let alone try to figure out where we are…"

"Maybe about 50 miles," said Max. "So on foot that would be something around 16 hours at max speed. With all this gear that we're going to have to haul, it'll be… who knows. A week, maybe? What about you?"

Georgia was surprised at how quickly the conversation had become normal. She knew now that Max and Mandy weren't a threat. They were like her. They would hurt people, but only to defend themselves. They would only use violence if they themselves were attacked, only if it was necessary.

Georgia thought back to how she'd made two attempts to steal, once from her neighbors, and once from the three women she'd become insta-friends with. She felt guilty about it, and neither attempt had gone well. She had the feeling that Max was too good of a guy to do something like that, to steal for his own benefit.

"I don't know," said Georgia. "We were heading up to a hunting cabin..."

"We?" said Max. "Who's we? Who else is with you?"

Georgia had been avoiding telling them that she had her kids, but the uneasiness she'd felt was gone now.

"I've got my two kids with me," she said. She pointed her flashlight into the trees where James and Sadie were hiding. She called out their names loudly.

After a few moments, James and Sadie emerged from the woods and came down to join them. Everyone introduced themselves.

Georgia noticed how cold and hungry they looked. They were younger than she was, and in some ways stronger, but they didn't have that mental toughness that adults gained with years and years of experience.

Maybe Georgia needed help. It would be a huge undertaking for her to bring James and Sadie on a long hike with pounds and pounds of gear. But could Max and Mandy help them? She didn't know how...

"We're going to have to hike it, definitely," said Max, coming back from looking under the Jeep.

Everyone was completely soaked.

"What do you say we set up a little camp?" said Georgia. "And get something to eat? We're not going to be able to carry all the food we've got, considering the other gear. And I imagine you might be just as hungry as we are."

"Sounds good," said Max. "Yeah, I feel like we've just been dealing with a constant string of obstacles since leaving. We've barely even had time to eat, let alone actually sit down and prepare a meal."

Georgia agreed, and they spent some time out in the storm trying to figure out what to do.

They thought of eating in the cars, but with the airbags deployed, with the sides smashed in, and the windows cracked and much of the glass completely shattered, the cars weren't the shelter that they'd been.

Max set to finding the perishable foods, some of which had already gone completely rotten and the rest of them went looking for a place among the trees that might provide some shelter. Normally, as Georgia knew, it was not good to be under trees when there was lightning. But they didn't have much choice. It was either stay out in the open on the street, and be miserable, being lashed by the elements, or risk it under the trees. The risk was small enough that it seemed worth it.

They found a place next to an outcropping of rock, some sort of boulder that had been sheared away by the eons of time. A pine tree was behind it, and it sheltered them somewhat. The rain still fell on them, but it was blocked by the thick boughs.

Max had a small camping stove, and the heat from it and the light was welcome. There wasn't much point in trying to start a fire, since it turned out that none of them were experts at camping skills.

While Georgia had spent a lot of time in the woods, it wasn't like she'd been making camp fires in a downpour. She'd always had gear with her.

Some of the food had already gone rotten, but most of it was still edible. There were steaks that had come from Max's freezer, apparently. They were now perfectly defrosted, and it seemed generous to Georgia that Max offered the first three steaks to Georgia and her kids.

The hot, seared meat tasted wonderful. They ate with their hands, like savages, like cave men in distant times. This was what the world was going to turn into—the savage lands where people ate like animals, the lands that once were. These lands would become again something resembling their distant glory, and their distant savageness. The rule of might would again become the rule of the land. The weak would perish, and for some the coming night would be nothing but a nightmare until a swift and painful end. But for others, it would be filled with glory and adventure. Modern life had cut everything off from its citizens—life was dull and filled with drudgery. In the modern world, there was no danger, not even a spark of it. There was nothing in the modern world to excite a man, or a woman, nothing except constant and mindless entertainment.

There was one thing that Georgia knew, and that was that she was going to be among the survivors. She and her children would survive. She wasn't sure about Chad, who sat apart from them, muttering to himself and shivering constantly. But Max and Mandy—they were like Georgia. They were going to survive too.

"Did you see that?" said Mandy.

"What?"

"There was something out there..."

"Where?"

"Out there... eyes... it looked like eyes in the night..." Mandy sounded scared. She seemed like a reasonable woman, but it was possible that she frightened easily. She didn't seem like the type who'd spent much time in the woods before.

"Probably just a raccoon or something," said Max.

"Do raccoon eyes... glow?" said Mandy.

"I don't know," said Max. He looked at Georgia for an answer. She could barely see his face in the flickering light of the little camp stove flame.

"I've never hunted raccoon," said Georgia.

"I think it was something else," said Mandy. "I think it was another person."

"Out there, now?"

J eremy was hunched over on his couch. He was tired and cold. The storm was relentless, pounding his midsize respectable house. He'd thought that he'd heard a tree falling in the back yard, but he'd been too terrified to even go look out the window.

Something was not right. Everything was very, very wrong.

It had been a couple days since the power had gone out. Maybe a day and a half? Jeremy wasn't sure. He didn't have his computer or phone to look at to check, and his memory was tiring, just like his body.

Jeremy had been on a good career path. He'd been proud of his career. He'd bought his first house just a year ago, the house he was now in. It wasn't fancy, but it was a good investment. Jeremy was proud that he'd done the right thing: gotten a job after college, worked his way up, saved his money. He'd bought things with credit cards to improve his credit score. He had money in the bank. He hadn't gone out to drink with his buddies to save money for his house. He hadn't gone golfing much to save money.

But despite his frugality, he'd made sure to spend money on the important things—expensive suits, for instance, so that he looked good when it became time for the promotions. He bought a good expensive mechanical watch, and then upgraded the band, because he'd read an article in a men's magazine about how a watch was an important feature in making a good first impression in business.

Jeremy thought back to the day at the office when the power had gone out. Looking back on it, Max had been right. His co-worker Max, who he'd been buddies with, wasn't like Jeremy at all. Recently, he'd been slacking off at work, even though it was known that the boss was looking for a new guy to promote. Jeremy had tried to convince Max to make a good impression, small things, like telling Max to sit up straighter, to actually pretend like he was interested in his work.

Jeremy had never been interested in his work, but that didn't matter to him. He'd managed to display such a great enthusiasm for his work, that over the years, he actually convinced even himself that he really did like crunching numbers all day long on a spreadsheet.

Max hadn't been anything like that, and there had been some change in Max at some point. Max had spent his time reading some kind of strange internet forum, and whenever Jeremy tried to talk to him, Max had seemed distant and far away. Occasionally Max would say cryptic things like, "You know it's all going to end, don't you?"

Jeremy would just laugh awkwardly, since he never knew how to handle things that were outside of his comfort zone.

Jeremy remembered how Max had left the office, and the boss had sworn up and down that he was fired.

It turned out that Max had been right. Things were changing, and not in a good way.

Jeremy hadn't gone back to work. There wasn't any way to. All the roads were blocked by the police, who were working closely with some military people. Jeremy thought they must have been with the national guard, but they never identified themselves, so he had no way of knowing who they were. There weren't markings on their trucks. Some of his neighbors had whispered that it was some kind of foreign invasion, but Jeremy didn't think so. He'd spoken to them, and they were definitely American, if accents and mannerisms were any way to judge.

Jeremy and his neighbors were stuck in their block, and food was already running low.

Jeremy ate all of his meals out. His freezer had a single frozen burrito from a year ago. His fridge only had condiments, for the occasions when he ordered take out instead of eating out.

He'd loved chain restaurants, and longed to go to his favorite now. There was literally nothing more in the world right now that he wanted more than a double dipped pile of deep fried cheese nachos. Well, that and for this whole mess to end right here and now.

Jeremy was a mental wreck. He'd been up all night through the storm. It was a little past dawn. The storm was still raging, but a small amount of weak light had passed through the clouds and Jeremy's house windows, allowing him to look around his living room at is possessions in pure terror.

Nothing here was of any use. He didn't own a single useful item. No firearms, no food, no survival gear whatsoever. His house was filled business books that he never read, ones that he thought would make him look intelligent if he were to ever have the boss over for dinner. Of course that had never happened. And it would certainly never happen now.

Something was wrong. Something was very wrong.

Military road blocks were not normal.

All communication was gone. Jeremy had checked his phone all through the night, hoping against hope that it would somehow miraculously work again. Of course, it was as dead as it had been since that day in the office.

Jeremy didn't know what to do. He had a vague idea of walking somewhere, avoiding the roadblock by cutting through a neighbor's lawn. Normally, he would never break the rules, but his stomach was rumbling. He wasn't used to going without regular meals, and his blood sugar was tanking, making him even more anxious than he otherwise would have been.

There was a loud noise that startled Jeremy out of his nightmarish daydream.

At first, Jeremy tried to ignore it. That was the best course of action, after all. Maybe it was just a noise from the storm.

But the sound continued, and gradually Jeremy grew aware of the fact that it must be a knock.

Someone was knocking, loudly.

Jeremy moved towards the door, walking as quietly as he could.

Thunder crashed outside. Lighting lit up the sky in the distance. But it was just light that Jeremy saw when he peeked through the blinds. The viewing angle didn't allow him to see who was at the door. Whoever it was was hidden behind one of the fancy posts that were only for decoration.

Jeremy considered his options. Whoever was at the door might be dangerous.

Jeremy considered going back to the kitchen for one of

the expensive kitchen knives that he never used, but thought better of it. He couldn't stomach the idea of stabbing someone, even if it was in his own defense.

He stood there, shaking, completely frozen with fear.

"I know you're in there," came a loud, unfamiliar voice, shouting over the storm.

Jeremy couldn't take it anymore. If he didn't open the door, someone might just break in, if that was what they wanted to do.

But if it was a neighbor, then there was no harm in opening the door.

Jeremy didn't know his neighbors, though, since he'd intentionally avoided them for years. He didn't like awkward conversations or small talk. For one thing, it wasn't good to waste time on things that weren't business related. And frankly, he didn't see much point in making any kind of social effort when that effort wasn't likely to propel him up the corporate ladder.

The shadow of a man moved in front of the outside window. Jeremy didn't see it until the lighting struck once more, illuminating the man from behind. He couldn't make out his features, but he was wiry and tall. He wasn't some hulking criminal who lifted weights. For some reason, Jeremy always imagined that criminals and people of bad intentions lifted weights and took steroids. He thought they were all huge, hulking beasts.

Jeremy took a deep breath. He threw the deadbolt back and with shaking hands, opened the door. He figured that most thin people were trustworthy. But even as he thought this, he knew that it was foolish. But the man could easily just break the window... Jeremy didn't want to have to deal with that.

Anyway, he was probably just overreacting, right? So the

power was out, and there was a military road block. But so what? There was no way that society could simply collapse, the way he feared it had. No, things were under control. They were always under control. Amway, the military was there. The police were nearby. That would deter any crime that might happen. There was no way some criminal would be foolish enough to commit a crime under the nose of the ample police force so close by.

"Hello?" said Jeremy, poking his head out as he opened the screen door.

The tall thin man turned towards him, and now that he was close, Jeremy saw him clearly in the dim early morning light. The man grinned a wide grin at him.

"Hi!" he said. "I don't think we've met, but I live right next door... Mind if I come in?"

"Uh," said Jeremy.

Jeremy wasn't used to thinking on his feet. He had an uneasy feeling about the man and his strange grin. But he wasn't good at saying "no." In fact, almost all his business training told him that he should never decline an invitation, never say no to anything at all. All of his business books, if he'd ever read them, echoed the same thing.

"Come on in," said Jeremy uneasily. But he tried to feign a smile nevertheless.

Lighting flashed behind the tall man as Jeremy led the way inside.

"What can I do for you?" said Jeremy, sitting back down on his couch. He was tired and standing was hurting his feet right now.

He gestured to an armchair cattycorner to the couch, but the tall man remained standing. He must have been at least six feet tall, maybe more. Jeremy studied his face as best he could while trying to meet the man in the eye. It was always good to look people in the eye. That was something Jeremy had drilled into his own head, and trained himself to do, despite how uncomfortable it made him feel. But it was a good business practice, and it had gotten him far at the office.

"Well," said the man. "We were running low on food over there, and I thought I'd come over to see if you had anything extra lying around..."

The man said he was a neighbor, but the more Jeremy thought about it, the more he was sure he had never seen the man in his life.

"Sorry," said Jeremy. "But I don't think I've seen you around."

"I work nights," said the man. "Always at work, basically. If I'm not, I'm asleep. Tough life, but it is what it is."

Jeremy nodded.

"Sorry," he said. "But I literally don't have a scrap of food in the house."

"Ah," said the man. "We're really hungry, though. Do you mind if I have a look? Maybe there's something you missed."

"Uh," said Jeremy. "I'm pretty sure there's nothing. I would have eaten it myself."

"But just a look?" said the man.

There was a strange look to his eyes. Either Jeremy was just noticing it, or the man's expression was changing, revealing his true character.

Jeremy was creeped out. He felt it in his stomach, a deep pit, a feeling of dread that simply wouldn't go away.

"I think I'm going to take a look anyway," said the man.

Jeremy didn't know if he should stop him. It wasn't like there was anything to find.

But he needed to stand up for himself. He knew that

clearly. If he let this guy walk all over him now, who knew what would come next.

"I'm afraid I wouldn't like that very much," said Jeremy, trying to couch his denial of the request in the most polite language he knew how to use.

The man started laughing. It was an eerie, horrible laugh.

He lifted the large raincoat he was wearing to reveal a pistol strapped in a holster to his belt. He took the pistol out slowly and carefully and held it in his hand, fondling it. He didn't point it at Jeremy, but the intention was clear.

"How about I do it anyway?" said the man.

"Uh," said Jeremy, his voice and body shaking from fear. "Sure, go ahead... Look, I don't want any problems. Take whatever you what."

The man disappeared into the kitchen, telling Jeremy to stay right where he was and not to move.

Jeremy didn't know what to do. Should he flee, run out the front door? But where to?

If only his favorite chain restaurant was open. It had always been his safe haven, his point of retreat during the lunch hour of a tough day at the office, when nothing seemed to go his way.

Jeremy had driven by there before the roadblock, and it was closed, without any lights on. There was no way it would be open now, even with the most dedicated employees imaginable. Without power, there wasn't anything. Nothing to eat. Nowhere to go.

Jeremy could hear the man rummaging around in his kitchen, knocking things over. He heard him tossing the pots and pans across the room, the ones that Jeremy had bought with his credit card but had never used.

The man returned within a couple minutes.

"No food," he muttered, looking at Jeremy with hunger in his eyes.

"I'm sure the power will come back on," said Jeremy. "This is just a little hiccup, you know?"

But he didn't even convince himself.

The man shook his head.

"It's over," he said.

The words echoed in Jeremy's memory. He'd heard someone else say those words. Recently. Now he remembered. It was Max. Max had said something like that at work.

Jeremy wondered what Max was doing now. Where had he rushed off to that day? How had he known that things would get so ugly so fast?

The man pulled the gun again from his holster and this time he pointed it at Jeremy.

"I know you're hiding something... something good..."

Jeremy raised his hands in the air in a gesture of surrender.

"I know you don't think I'm really your neighbor," said the man, his gun hand shaking slightly. "But it's true, and I've got a family to feed. They're hungry, and it's only going to get worse. It's every man for himself from now on. I've worked double and even triple shifts for years. I've held down two jobs at once. But you... I've watched you come and go, even when you haven't seen me. It's when I'm lying awake in the day, when I can't sleep because of the light coming in and I can't even afford to buy black out curtains. It doesn't happen often, because usually I'm dead tired and I fall asleep... But sometimes the light and the anxiety gets to me. And I peek through my blinds and I see you... I see you in your fancy new car..."

Jeremy thought of his car. It wasn't much good to him

now, since the gas tank was empty. Even if the road blockade wasn't there, he wouldn't get far if gas stations didn't work. He'd stopped at one on the way home from work that day, and he'd found that there wasn't anything he could do to activate the pump. No matter which credit card he'd tried, the power was out and there was nothing to do about it.

"I see you in that car, your perfect house, while mine's in shambles... I know you've got money. You must have food somewhere, or water. It's just a little bit of hunger now, just a little nibble, but it's going to grow. The hunger's going to grow in the bellies of my children and there's nothing that's going to stop it... I don't want to do this, but I'm prepared to kill you if it means giving food to my kids."

"Please," said Jeremy. "There's no need to kill me... I'll give you whatever you want..."

"Food," said the man. "Water. Guns. Medical supplies."

Jeremy had none of these.

He didn't know what to say. If he said "no," the man would think he was lying, and possibly shoot him in the arm or something to cause him enough pain to make him speak.

"I don't know what to say," said Jeremy.

"Do you have it or not?" said the man.

"I don't," said Jeremy.

The gun was pointed at him and he was experiencing the most anxiety and terror of his entire life. He'd never felt this bad, as if a hollow hole of dread was opening in his stomach, trying to swallow the rest of his body.

"Shit," said the man, putting the gun down on the coffee table. He put his head in his hands and started emitting strange sounds.

Soon, Jeremy realized that the man was sobbing.

That was a dramatic turn of events, thought Jeremy to himself.

"I don't know what I'm going to do," said the man. "I have to feed my kids. And everything's just so screwed up. It's all screwed. I don't know what we're going to do. I can't let them starve."

"I'm sure things are going to start happening again," said Jeremy. "I'm sure this isn't the end. I mean, that would be completely crazy, right? That's what happens in the movies and stuff. But this is real life, and the people in power wouldn't let that sort of thing happen to us. They wouldn't let us just fall off a cliff like that."

There was a loud sound outside, the sound of heavy trucks rolling slowly down the street. Jeremy could hear the tires heavy on the pavement and the engines rumbling over the sound of the storm.

"Sounds like someone's outside," said Jeremy.

He moved over to the window to see what was going on. He peered through the blinds.

What he saw next scared him even more than having a gun pointed at him.

The military trucks, the same type as the ones from the road blockade, had stopped right in front of his house. They'd parked in the middle of the street, their engines still running.

Two soldiers, both with machine guns, or whatever they were (Jeremy didn't know anything about firearms) were approaching his house, walking slowly and purposefully.

There was a knock on the door.

Jeremy knew better than to ignore the knock.

"Hello?" he said, opening the door. He was too terrified to say anything else. He wanted to ask, though, about the state of affairs that they were in. His mind was full of anxious questions.

He was torn between two positions. On one hand, he looked to the soldiers as the upholders of peace and justice. He believed that they would be the ones who protected himself and the other good citizens from chaos. He believed that they'd be the ones responsible for eventually restoring order. But he also feared them. He knew that they were men just like himself, and that... well, things might go south quickly if he disobeyed them.

"Food," said one of the soldiers.

"Food?" said Jeremy, trying to stall as best he could.

"We need food. We're requiring food from the neighborhood."

"I'm sorry," said Jeremy. "But I just don't have any. I really wish I did. And if I did, you'd be the first ones I'd give it to."

Both soldiers glared at him.

Then one pointed his gun right at Jeremy's chest.

"Step aside. We're going to check the house."

Jeremy moved to the side.

The soldiers brushed past him as if he was completely insignificant and meaningless.

"Drop the weapon!" they shouted upon entering the living room.

Jeremy followed the soldiers into the living room, moving out of the alcove, but he kept himself as close to the door as possible.

The soldiers were pointing their guns at Jeremy's neighbor, the man he'd never met before.

The neighbor had a crazed look on his face. Jeremy had already seen him go from grinning, to terrifying, to crying. Now he seemed to have entered a new phase of emotions, nothing but insanity showing on his face. But it wasn't insanity. It was desperation, nothing but a normal reaction to an extreme situation.

The neighbor already had his gun in his hand and was pointing it at the soldiers.

The soldiers didn't bother giving another order, waiting to see if he would obey. They were in the mindset of shooting first and not bothering to ask questions later. They held their guns in a practiced manner, not budging from their spots. Their gazes were steely. They wore body armor. Their camouflage fatigues bristled with gear, extra ammo, water bottles, even grenades.

They opened fire at the same time, spraying bullets at the neighbor.

The neighbor got off one single shot. Jeremy wasn't sure, in the end, when he thought about it later, who'd fired first. No matter how he reconstructed it in his head, it didn't seem to make sense.

But the soldiers must have fired first. They must have. But then how did his neighbor get off that single shot?

The neighbor missed. The soldiers were unharmed.

Jeremy felt a flash of searing pain in his leg.

The bullet from his neighbor had lodged itself there.

Jeremy screamed and tried to grab his leg, and toppled over onto the ground.

The soldiers looked at him momentarily, and then stepped over him to walk through the living room into the kitchen.

Jeremy lay on the floor in complete agony. His vision had gone somewhat blurry. He couldn't think straight.

He was only vaguely aware of when the soldier came back into the room, empty handed of course, since there wasn't a scrap of food in the house.

They stood over him and looked at him, grumbling.

One of them took something out of his pocket and applied it to Jeremy's leg. It was probably one of those quick clot systems that stopped bleeding.

Jeremy tried to speak, but nothing but tears and moaning came out. He couldn't get a single word out, let alone string together a sentence.

The soldiers grabbed him. One took an arm each, and they dragged him outside into the rain. Jeremy was instantly soaked. The crashing of thunder surrounded him.

They dragged him into one of the vehicles, and there, he lost consciousness.

27

MAX

The next day when they woke at sunrise, the storm had blown over, leaving the woods pristine and perfect looking. The sun was shining brightly and there wasn't a cloud in the sky.

Max went over in his mind what had happened the night before. They'd eaten their first good meal in a long time. Max's stomach was still feeling full from all the steak he'd consumed the night before. He'd even had a beer, one that Georgia had given him.

Despite the way meeting Georgia and her family had started, tensions were almost non-existent now.

Max liked Georgia and her kids. She wasn't a malicious person. He could tell that right from the beginning. She was like him, just doing what she thought she had to do.

The others were still sleeping, in their wet clothes that were starting to dry.

Max seemed to be the only one awake.

He got up, a little stiff from sleeping out in the open on the forest floor.

He looked down at them. Georgia, Mandy, James, and Sadie were all curled up into little balls.

Chad... where was Chad?

Max started circling the little camp, moving in larger and larger circles until he found him.

Chad was wide awake, looking like he hadn't slept the entire night.

"How you holding up, Chad?" said Max. He hoped that Chad was going to be coherent, at the least. He was seriously starting to lose his patience with his old friend.

"Hey," said Chad. He sounded lucid, yet really down. He didn't sound like the exuberant party boy he'd been earlier.

"How you feeling?"

"Not bad," said Chad. "The withdrawal is starting to calm down a lot. I couldn't sleep all last night, but I'm... I don't know. I'm feeling better."

Max nodded.

"I can't remember the last time I wasn't loaded," said Chad. "It's been... I don't know... ages and ages. I should have quit that shit years ago. Maybe this is a wake up call for me, I don't know."

"I think it's a wakeup call for humanity," said Max. "Can you walk?"

"I think so."

"Come with me to check out the cars. It'll give you something to do."

They walked the short distance to the road where the cars still were.

"They're smashed up pretty good," said Chad.

Max nodded. "There's no way they're going to run."

Max still had the keys to the Jeep in his pocket, where they would serve merely as a reminder of the life he once had.

"I was hoping to use the battery," said Max. "And maybe some of the other mechanical pieces. I thought they could be useful in the future. But it looks like it's all going to stay here. We'll just have to carry what we can on our backs."

There were still plenty of supplies loaded in the Jeep, and the SUV.

Max suddenly realized that he'd made a grave error last night—he should have been protecting the gear. But he'd been so fatigued, simply so tired, that they must not have been thinking straight.

But fortunately it seemed as if no one else had come along in the night to rob them.

Max remembered that last night Mandy had said she'd thought she'd seen something, some pair of eyes out in the darkness.

It sent a shiver of terror through him, but Max shook off the thought. It was probably just some animal, or maybe nothing at all.

"So," said Chad. "I don't remember much of last night. But it seems like we're now friends with the people who drove right into us and destroyed the Jeep."

"Yup," said Max. "It's not really their fault, you know."

"So what's the plan? We're going to walk to the farm house?"

"Yeah," said Max. "If you want to come, that is."

Chad didn't say anything for a moment. "I was ready to die," he said. "I just wanted to enjoy the high for a little while longer. Honestly, my plan was never to come to the farm with you. I figured I would just get out at some point along the road and walk over a cliff or something. Not that I'd really figured much of it out yet... But now that I'm not high, well, things seem a lot different. So yeah, I'd like to come, if you'll have me. I know I haven't been a good friend over the years, and I haven't been much help so far on this trip."

Max studied him. He knew that sober Chad was a completely different person than high Chad.

"It'll be good to have you along," he said. "But it's going to be a lot of work. We're going to have to fight for our survival once we get there."

Chad nodded. "I'm ready for that," he said. "A fresh start is what I need... Could be the best rehabilitation program ever, really."

Max chuckled a little. "We all need a fresh start," he said. "We've been living hollow lives for too long, hollow little lives borrowed on credit. We knew deep inside that this day would come..."

Chad nodded slowly.

"So what's with you and Mandy," he said. "She's your girlfriend or something?"

"Wow, you must have been really out of it," said Max. "No, she was my neighbor. I'd seen her before, but we'd never spoken. I ended up shooting some guys who were trying to rape her. I would have thought that would have been the kind of thing you would have remembered, Chad."

"Well, I was pretty out of it," said Chad. "If I'm good at one thing, it's getting high, really really high, and staying high."

"You're strong," said Max. "You don't realize it yet, but under that layer of fat you've been carrying about for years, there are muscles that want to work, muscles that want to work hard to eke out a living on the land."

Chad laughed vaguely. "We'll see about that," he said. "I can only promise one thing, and that's that I'll try."

"Good," said Max. "Let's go wake up the others. We've

got to get some food and then hit the trail as soon as we can."

"So the new people are coming with us?" said Chad. "How's that going to work?"

Max shook his head. "Georgia said she's taking her kids to some hunting cabin," he said. "I don't know where it is, but I imagine we'll be parting ways today."

Chad nodded.

Max and Chad made their way back to the campsite, where everyone was slowly waking up.

Mandy was the most awake, and she already had the stove going, preparing some instant coffee as well as two dozen eggs. "I thought they'd just go bad anyway," she said.

"You're right," said Max. "We've got to start eating the perishable food as soon as we can. There's no point in waiting. And we've got to remember to eat. We've gone too long strung out on hunger. It makes us create errors and problems. We've got to stay well rested and well fed, at least as much as possible, from here on out."

"That sounds nice," said Mandy. "That was the first time I've slept properly since leaving. Oh, and I've looked at the maps already."

Max nodded. He was pleased that she was so useful, and taking so much initiative. It was good that he'd brought her along. He thought back to the time when he was considering whether or not to enter her apartment. Now, he was glad that he'd done it. At the time, it had felt like a terrible, terrible decision.

Mandy served the eggs to everyone. There weren't any plates, so some ate the eggs off of pages of the atlas map, doing their best to keep the paper flat like a plate.

Max simply took the scrambled eggs in his cupped hands

and ate them quickly. He sat on a rock, slightly apart from everyone else, watching them, and considering what would lie in store for them in the days ahead. This was a turning point, with the loss of the Jeep. But maybe it was good. The Jeep had to go sooner or later, considering the gas situation. And it had been a mental crutch for Max, a piece of his old life that he hadn't wanted to give up. Better to get it over with in a single crash, like pulling a bandage quickly off of a painful wound.

Mandy and Georgia were huddled over the maps, discussing their routes.

Chad was off on his own, a serious expression on his face.

Georgia's children, James and Sadie, were sitting by their mother.

From where he sat, Max could hear the conversation.

"So I think I know where we are now," said Mandy. "And it looks like your hunting cabin is on the way to where we're headed."

Georgia grinned. "What do you say, Max?" she called out. "Are we coming with you, or are we just going to slow you down?"

"Better if we all go together," said Max.

Now that they knew where they were headed, and it had been decided that everyone would go together until they reached the hunting cabin, they spent most of their time sorting through all the gear and food.

It was a big job, because in both vehicles, everything had been stuffed together in a very haphazard manner.

Max was dismayed to realize what he'd thrown out when he'd picked up Chad, to make room for him. It had been some food, but that wasn't the worst of it. He'd inadvertently thrown out a bag full of ammunition, a bag full of medical supplies, and other odds and ends that he'd thought would be useful for surviving.

They had enough food for the hike and even after that. Even though there were a lot of them, the food was plentiful. Georgia had brought along a lot of food as well. For the most part, the parties kept their gear separate from one another. Georgia and her children carried most of their belongings, and Max, Mandy, and Chad carried their own things.

It turned out that Chad's big frame could carry a huge amount. Of course, he would tire easily, because of his own extra weight that he was carrying, all those pounds of fat. Max warned him of this, and cautioned him to carry less gear. But Chad seemed determined to "pull his weight" among the group as it were, and he loaded himself with many extra things that might be useful.

Max lent Georgia and her children extra hiking backpacks. So they each had a large hiking backpack with gear strapped all over it.

Max carried a lot of weight himself. To repay him for loaning her the packs, Georgia lent Max's party a rifle.

Initially, Georgia offered the gun to Mandy, but Mandy said she didn't know how to use it.

"I'll take it," Max had said. He was familiar with rifles as well as handguns, even though he didn't have his own. It was, by his own admission, a huge oversight in his planning.

In the end, Georgia had enough rifles for everyone. She didn't want to leave them behind in her SUV, so despite Mandy's protests, Georgia lent her one, as well as Chad. Georgia's own children carried rifles, although it was clear that while her son knew how to use one, her daughter, Sadie held the gun awkwardly and at a great distance from herself, as if she was nervous of it.

So they looked like a very strange group of hikers, each with a gun.

But they were ready, and as they walked away from the cars, Max felt a sort of relief washing over him. Gone were the days of clinging to the past, to automobiles and machines.

It wasn't as if Max was a Luddite. In fact, he appreciated technology and what it had done for his own life. It had made him comfortable. But he was practical, and he'd always understood the limitations of technology.

Mandy led the way, and Georgia walked beside her through the woods. Mandy knew the route, and was good with maps. She held a compass as she walked, and consulted it frequently.

Without Mandy, Max didn't know what would have happened to him. Maybe he would have gotten lost. Maybe he would have tried to fight his way out of situations that couldn't be fought out of. If he'd run into those villagers earlier, maybe he would have engaged them in a firefight where he would have been clearly outnumbered. He would have died. Or maybe he never would have even reached that little town... He didn't know, and he put the thoughts aside, realizing that there was no point now in speculating about what could have happened. All he knew was that he was grateful for Mandy. And in the future, maybe he would be grateful for having Chad along.

He was surprised how well the two parties mingled together. There was a natural sort of trust that had established itself last night around the meal, and the party chatted amicably as they walked.

After Mandy and Georgia, James and Sadie followed at a short distance. Chad walked behind them, loaded down with gear, swearing up a storm, and grunting with each step.

Max followed behind everyone else, keeping some distance between himself and Chad. He kept his eyes and ears open for sounds around him. If there was anyone else out here, even though the possibility was remote, he wanted to see them first.

He kept his rifle ready in front of him, his finger laying along the trigger guard, with the safety off.

Bits and pieces of the conversation from Mandy and Georgia drifted back to Max, but he didn't pay it much attention unless it was something practical.

It was good, thought Max, that they'd met Georgia. Without her, they wouldn't be armed as they were now.

He hoped they wouldn't encounter someone else out here, but the possibility was always there. He knew that he needed to expect the unexpected.

The trees looked gorgeous with the sun streaming down through the branches. It had been a long time since Max had been to this remote part of Pennsylvania, but he already liked it. It wasn't a bad place to set up a nice life, not bad at all.

The going was somewhat tough, because they weren't on any sort of path. They'd decided to cut right through the forest, rather than take the road. There were a few reasons for this. For one, Mandy had assured everyone that she knew how to get there through woods. There was supposedly a hiking path that they could take. They only had a mile or two to go until they reached it, and they could take that part of the way as they continued north. Cutting through the woods would shave many hours off their trip. They figured that they had about two days of hiking to get to the farmhouse, and maybe a day to get to the hunting cabin.

The main reason that Max liked walking through the

woods instead of taking the road was that they had much less of a chance of running into anyone.

If people were starting to leave the cities and suburbs, they would come out here, and they would surely be in cars —the people who made it here already, that is. In the future, there would come the hordes of slowly walking masses, moving like zombies in low budget movies, looking for anything to eat, and willing to do anything to get what they needed.

Max's mind turned to his future life, and what it would be like.

He had some vague plans, but when he tried to think concretely about what he would do, he drew some huge blanks that worried him.

His whole purpose now was to get there, to get to the farmhouse. But once there, how would life settle out? What would the day-to-day routine look like?

He supposed that he would live there with Mandy and Chad.

He looked ahead and caught sight of Mandy's rear end, as she walked in her jeans. She was an attractive woman, and Max realized for the first time that he was attracted to her *as* a woman. It wasn't just her body that drew him to her, but the growing awareness he had of her personality. She'd started the journey in the worst possible way. She'd been completely unaware, and perhaps even unwilling to accept what had happened. But now she seemed to embrace the situation and she was willing to do whatever necessary to survive. Max appreciated that kind of attitude.

She would make a good partner at the farmhouse. He had a feeling that she would accept him. He'd seen the glances she'd given him here and there. They weren't quite glances of longing, or romantic interest, because the situation was so intense that it simply didn't allow for things like that. But there was something there in her gaze, something like respect and understanding.

Maybe they could create a family there on the farm. Maybe Max could unearth some ancient farm equipment and get the farm producing food again. It would be a massive undertaking, with a host of complicated obstacles. The main one, thought Max, was that there were no farm animals there. But maybe in the coming months and years, it would somehow be possible to get them. After all, animals had a way of surviving even when humans couldn't.

28

When Jeremy woke up, the pain was even worse, if that was possible, than the moment that he'd been shot.

He immediately thought: there's no way I'm going to survive this. He figured there was simply no way he could go on with the pain, and medical treatment, well, he didn't think that was going to happen.

But maybe... maybe it would. After all, just because the power was out, it wasn't as if the doctors had disappeared, right?

The soldiers had been harsh with him, sure. They had dragged him off. But they had, after all, treated him somewhat. They had stopped the bleeding, and he was alive, whereas if they'd left him there he would be dead.

Maybe they'd just been following orders. Maybe they'd been under orders to get food at whatever cost. The military needed to be fed just like the citizens. And if peace, law, and order were going to continue to reign supreme, then feeding the military and police could be considered of the utmost importance.

Jeremy was vaguely aware of his surroundings. He knew he was somewhere with a lot of other people. His vision was blurry as he looked around, and something had happened to his glasses. He saw just a blurry mass of people. It might have been the same day, or maybe the next. He wasn't sure, and he didn't know how to tell.

But without his vision being as good as it should have been, he still knew there were many, many people. He could hear them, their cries of pain and their moans of hunger. He could smell them, the pungent human smell of many, many unwashed bodies.

Jeremy sat up despite the pain. He pulled up his khaki pant leg that was stained with dried blood. He looked at his wound. As he'd suspected, the soldiers had put some kind of field-treatment military medical supply on it. It looked like a white patch, a large bandage, that stuck to his skin with some kind of glue. It was completely soaked through with a rich red blood, but the bleeding seemed to have stopped.

Jeremy didn't dare try to stand up. He knew that he would never be able to. His leg hurt too much. Simply too much. He had to grit his teeth just to stand as he sat there in a crouched position.

"Hey," said Jeremy. It seemed to take all of his strength to speak. His stomach rumbled horribly at him. His leg ached. His whole body ached.

The woman next to him, who he could see fairly well, ignored him.

"Excuse me," said Jeremy. He reached out and tugged at her sleeve.

"Get away from me!" she cried at him, pulling her arm violently away from him.

"I'm not going to hurt you," said Jeremy. "But can you tell me where we are? What's going on?"

"What's going on? I'll tell you what's going on. And it's not good."

She paused and didn't say anything.

"Tell me," said Jeremy desperately. He didn't know how much longer he could hold this "conversation" that he was having. His mouth and throat were parched, and each word seemed to only cause him more pain. "Tell me what's happening. Where are we? I don't seem to have my glasses."

"Your glasses?" laughed the woman. "You're not going to get them back. You're not going to get anything back."

She was a woman in her early forties, only a few years older than Jeremy himself. But she looked much older. Maybe it was that the makeup she'd been wearing had smeared and run. It looked as if she had been crying intensely. And where there was no makeup, her skin looked like that of a much older woman.

The sight of her face close up scared Jeremy. Maybe he was starting to hallucinate, he thought. Maybe he was seeing things. Maybe he was going crazy. Maybe this was all just a dream.

Wouldn't that have been a relief? If this horrible situation, with all these moaning people around him—if it was all just the fantasy of a man gone insane, a man whose brain could no longer support the rigors of modern culture.

Someone was approaching with heavy footsteps.

It was a soldier.

"Identify yourself," he said, stopping right in front of Jeremy.

When Jeremy didn't immediately answer, the man pointed his gun right at Jeremy's chest.

Jeremy almost didn't answer. If he could just get shot now, that would be a relief. If he could just end it now... That was all he wanted, for this nightmare to end. He no longer cared *how* it ended. He just wanted it to be over. He would have liked it to end, and to be back at the comfortable air conditioned office. But death... that didn't sound too bad right now. It was an end, after all. At least it was that.

"Your name!" screamed the soldier, leaning down a little to scream directly into Jeremy's face. Jeremy saw the face and it looked horrible. It was a normal face, but it was marred by fear and a thousand ugly emotions all competing for space. The soldier shoved the muzzle of his gun into Jeremy's chest. It hurt terribly, and Jeremy fell down onto his back.

"Jeremy Gibbons," said Jeremy, speaking with pain.

"Empty your pockets," said the solider.

Jeremy didn't act immediately. He was a little dazed, very confused, and didn't seem to understand the directions well.

"The woman at his side started cackling. "He wants your money," she said. "But he knows it won't do him any good. Not now. Not ever..."

"Shut up," shouted the solider at her, pointing his gun at her instead of Jeremy.

"You know you can't do anything with that money," said the woman, speaking unnecessarily loudly. Her words seemed to echo inside of Jeremy's head, hurting his brain, his eardrums, his whole body. Her voice had a shrill tone to it that seemed to reverberate against Jeremy's bones.

"Shut up," yelled the soldier. His voice was a mixture of anger and fear.

Without another word, his finger gripped the trigger, and he unleashed a hail of bullets that splattered against the woman's chest.

Blood spurted out, and Jeremy watched in horror as the woman fell down on the ground, lifeless. Her chest was ripped open by a dozen bullets.

Jeremy was frozen. The solider pointed his gun directly at Jeremy. Jeremy knew what he wanted, but he couldn't seem to make his arms move. He was paralyzed with fear. No matter how much he wanted to give the solider his wallet, give him everything in his pockets, his arms simply wouldn't obey his brain. And, honestly, part of him wanted to die. Part of him wanted to die right then and there. It would be easier.

But before the soldier could shoot him, heavy footsteps were coming. Jeremy could feel the vibrations on the earth. For the first time, his tired brain registered that he was lying on damp earth. He was on some kind of football field. Maybe he was at the high school football stadium? Had he and all these other people been brought here to form some kind of detention center?

The man approached from the side, flanked by six soldiers, three on each side.

He was a huge man, towering above everyone else, with a wide face and close-cropped hair. He looked like a soldier, but he wore civilian clothes. He was armed with only a handgun worn openly on a holster. His muscles bulged in his tight t-shirt. He must have been some kind of military commander.

The soldier froze as he saw the men approach.

"Johnson!" called the big man with the wide face. "What the hell do you think you're doing?"

"Nothing," replied Johnson the soldier.

"He was robbing another one of them," shouted one of the commander's sidekicks.

"I wasn't," said Johnson, but his voice betrayed him, showing his fear and his guilt.

"Spoils go to the commander, Johnson," said the commander. "You know that, don't you? I suppose you're going to say that you were going to bring them to me, weren't you?"

Jeremy thought that this couldn't possibly be true. It had only been a couple days, right? Or else he'd been passed out for longer than he'd thought. After all, he had no way of knowing what day it was. Or even week... although he supposed that there was no way he could have survived over a week without food or water.

But had society really already come to this, to some horrible nightmarish version of a free for all, where the mighty ruled? It simply couldn't be true.

Before Johnson could answer, the commander shouted.

The soldiers who flanked him moved out and grabbed Johnson savagely. One of them took his gun, and another hit Johnson in the stomach with a vicious uppercut. Johnson doubled over in pain as two men dragged him off.

Jeremy lay frozen in fear, hoping no one would notice him.

But that turned out to be too much to wish for.

The commander himself grabbed Jeremy and dragged him. He was strong and Jeremy didn't weigh that much. He was dragged easily by his shirt collar through the field that had become mud.

What Jeremy saw horrified him. The field was completely full of men, women, and children, in various states of disrepair and distress. Jeremy couldn't see far, but the field was packed full of people, and as he was dragged along, he got a blurry yet close up view of many of them.

What would happen to these people? There didn't seem to be any water or food. Would they simply all starve or die of thirst?

After being dragged across the width of the field, Jeremy was thrown roughly to the ground. This area was muddier than the rest.

Jeremy was right next to a pile of bodies lying face down in the mud. They were stacked one on top of another. Blood seeped out of some of them. The smell was horrible, and Jeremy's body tried to vomit instinctively. But he couldn't do it. Only some yellow bile came up, leaving a horrible taste in his mouth, and dribbling down his chin onto his shirt.

Jeremy was next to the soldier who'd tried to rob him. Both were lying in the mud. The solider made no move to get up. Jeremy was too fatigued to even try, and in too much pain. He knew the end was near, and he wasn't going to fight it. He didn't have the will to live, the burning desire required to make things work.

There was nothing to say. There was nothing read to them. There was no explanation of why they were being executed. But it was clear what was happening, what was going to happen. It was as clear as the day.

Jeremy vaguely knew that the day would continue without him, that the world would still exist without him. But he didn't care. He didn't have the energy for complicated thought. He just wanted an end. It was a selfish end, but then again, he'd lived a thoroughly selfish life. A lazy life, the life of a coward, hiding behind his machines and his money and his good credit.

The soldiers were in front of them. They raised their guns and Jeremy saw in slow motion as they pulled their triggers.

A hail of bullets exploded out of them. The body of the soldier named Johnson danced in the mud as the bullets riddled him with violent holes.

Jeremy was next, and he made no protest. He simply waited for his turn.

The path was tough, and the minutes seemed to stretch into hours. Georgia was worried about her children carrying so much gear with them, such heavy packs. But they held up quite well, and their spirits seemed to be good.

The sun made it all possible. If the storm had continued, or if the sky had been filled with clouds, it would have been much more difficult to marshal the morale necessary for the long trek.

"Only a little while longer until we hit the trail," said Mandy, who had the maps out in front of her, along with the compass.

Georgia didn't say anything. Mandy had been saying the same thing for what felt like all day.

Georgia really hoped Mandy knew what she was doing. For all Georgia knew, they could be headed in the opposite direction of where they were supposed to be heading. She hoped against hope that that wasn't the case.

Max had been bringing up the rear, and he sped up a little to join Georgia, who dropped a little behind Mandy, because there wasn't always enough room to walk three by three through the woods.

Behind them, her children were silent, their footsteps as light as they could be with their heavy packs. But Chad was making an enormous amount of noise, his sneakers crashing down onto the forest floor heavily. Each step sounded like a herd of elephants. He wheezed and he huffed and puffed with exertion. But there was something new about his attitude. Even Georgia, who didn't know him well at all, could sense the change. He was silent as he struggled. He kept on, and he didn't curse and he didn't complain. He simply kept going. He simply did what needed to be done.

"How are you holding up?" said Max.

Georgia had known for a while that she liked Max. Not in a romantic way, obviously, but just as a person. He seemed to have something about him... some quality. He had what it took to survive. It was something almost indescribable. Georgia had an idea that she herself possessed pieces of these qualities. Max seemed to have the whole package. In another time, he could have been a leader of something great.

"Good," said Georgia.

"And your kids?" said Max.

"They're doing as well as can be expected," said Georgia.

"You know we can hear you, right?" said Sadie.

Georgia ignored her.

"What do you think about this hiking trail?" said Max, in a voice quiet enough that Mandy was unlikely to hear it.

Georgia lowered her own voice. "I don't know," she said. "She's been saying all day that we're close. I'm starting to have my doubts."

"Me too," said Max. "It's not that it's necessary, but if we don't come across it, it could mean that we're not where we think we are."

"And obviously that could pose problems," said Georgia.

"No kidding," said Max. "I'm going to talk to Mandy about it."

Max picked up his pace to join Mandy up in front.

Georgia walked closer to them so that she could over-hear what they were saying. She didn't think they would mind, and, plus, she had more important things on her mind than being polite. Survival trumped social niceties.

"No," Mandy was saying. "I'm sure it's up here. Trust me, Max, I know where I'm going. It's just a little farther."

"Is it possible we're not where you think we are?" said Max. He said it in a calm tone. He wasn't being accusatory. He just legitimately needed to know what the situation was.

"No," said Mandy. "The only possibilities are that we're a little farther south that I'd thought. Or the trail might have grown over. It is an old map."

Georgia was keeping her eyes peeled for any trail makers. So far, she hadn't seen anything that looked remotely familiar to her, even though she'd been to this area before.

"Hey," said Georgia, suddenly spotting something. "Look! A trail marker."

It was there, a spray-painted blue mark on a larger tree trunk.

"Yes!" said Mandy excitedly. "I knew it."

"Good," said Max, nodding.

He moved ahead of the rest of them. It was amazing to Georgia that he could move so quickly with all the gear that he was carrying. He didn't seem as tired as the rest of them. He must have been in even better shape than he looked.

Max paused at the trail, waiting for the rest of them to catch up.

Georgia arrived next, then her children, and finally, after what seemed like an eternity, Chad arrived, crashing through the underbrush, wheezing heavily.

"Looks like the trail grew over a little," said Max.

Sure enough, the trail wasn't exactly what you'd call a hiking trail. There were plants growing where it would have been a clear path a few years ago.

"It's only a couple years of growth," said Georgia, examining it. "It'll still be easier to walk through this, and we can walk three at a time. That would make me feel like we had a little more security."

"Which way are we headed, Mandy?" said Max.

Mandy pointed in the direction that would take them north.

"Let's take a break for lunch," said Max. "I know we're all tired, and we could use a rest. I know I could really use one myself."

Georgia knew that it wasn't quite true. Max didn't really need a break. He was strong, and he didn't seem as tired of the rest of them. He must have had a very regimented training schedule in the years before this event. Georgia knew that Max was doing this, encouraging a break, so that the rest of them didn't get too tired. In her opinion, he was being an excellent leader.

They sat down in a close circle right on the trail, as Max cleared away some of the overgrown branches here and there, so that they could sit more comfortably. Max worked tirelessly with a large knife that he kept on his belt. He refused all offers of help, and encouraged them all to start preparing the food.

There was still some perishable food left. Some chicken

that had been frozen, for instance, that wasn't yet too rotten to eat.

Georgia helped Mandy start the cook stove. Georgia knew that they couldn't rely on it forever. There simply wasn't enough gas. But fortunately, she knew well how to make a fire, provided the conditions were good. Max had all manner of camping equipment, like flint and steel fire starters, that would last a long, long time. He had enough to start fires for many years to come. Georgia, on the other hand, had a couple of lighters with her as their supplies. Those wouldn't last more than a few months if she was lucky. She envied the supplies that Max had. Although, then again, he didn't have the firepower that Georgia had brought along.

When Max had finished cutting away the branches, he came over to Georgia.

"Georgia, could I have a word with you?"

"Sure," she said, getting up. "You're fine with the rest of it, Mandy?"

"I think maybe Sadie can give me a hand."

To Georgia's surprise, Sadie was happy to have something to do. She set to work with Mandy, cooking the food and figuring out how to distribute it to everyone.

It made Georgia happy and proud to see her daughter doing something useful, and to apparently take pleasure in doing so. Sadie still carried her broken phone with her, but she no longer checked it. It was a necessary change in attitude, and Georgia was finally able to see it. Maybe the version of Sadie who'd saved them from the McKinneys' was returning. Sadie was growing up, perhaps more quickly than she would have otherwise done. It was a good change.

Georgia followed Max away from the group, back into the denseness of the woods, away from the trail.

"I wanted to ask you something," said Max in a low voice, so they wouldn't be overheard.

"Shoot," said Georgia.

"I've been thinking about our destinations," said Max. "I was so focused on just getting out of the chaos. It seems like, well I don't want to speak too soon, but it seems like we've been through the worst of it for now. There might be more challenges ahead."

Georgia nodded. Even over the short course of time that she'd known Max, she had a lot of respect for him. She was willing to listen to whatever he had to say.

"I feel the same way," said Georgia. "While we were walking today, I started thinking about what the future holds for my family."

Max nodded, listening carefully. "Me, too," he said. "I've been trying to picture what life will be like at the farm house. I think the only way to really make it is to have some kind of agricultural system. You know, get the old farm working again. I'll need to somehow get some animals, and plant crops. I feel confident that while those are going to be big challenges, there's some way to overcome them. There'll be some way to get the animals, and some way to get the seeds."

"It does sound difficult," said Georgia.

"But what I realized," said Max. "Is that it's going to require a huge amount of man power. A huge amount of work, human hours of labor. So I'll just lay it on the line for you. Here's what I'm proposing: that you and your kids come and live on the farm with me, Mandy, and Chad. It's not going to be easy. It's going to be a hard road ahead, but I think it's going to be easier if we all work together."

Georgia liked the idea immediately. After all, she'd been preoccupied with how she and her kids were going to live.

Basically her plan involved hunting for food. But she knew that there would be other problems that would crop up. There would be fresh potable water to obtain. There would be medical emergences. Plus, the biggest threat to their safety could be the invading hordes that would come from the cities, tired and hungry and willing to try anything to survive. They would have a better chance of surviving if they were with Max.

"OK," said Georgia. "I like it."

"That was fast," said Max, laughing.

"Well," said Georgia. "When you hear a good plan, you've just got to go with it. We can work out the details over time."

"We've got a ton of work ahead of us," said Max. "And what I'm hoping now is that the place is in OK condition. We'll have to work out the particulars as we go, I guess."

Georgia nodded.

Suddenly, Max looked over her shoulder, deep into the woods.

"Turn around and look," whispered Max. "I think we've got company."

Georgia turned quickly so as not to miss it.

It was something way off in the distance, partly hidden behind a tree. It moved quickly, and if it hadn't had been for Max pointing it out to her, she might have thought that she'd imagined it. But even if she couldn't make out the object clearly, it was clear what it was. It was a bright red shirt, a color that certainly didn't exist naturally in the forest.

It was another human.

Another human following them.

They were back on the trail after having eaten.

Despite having sat down and rested, despite being well fed, they were all still tired. And there was a lot of grumbling and groaning as they got back on the trail, walking ahead.

Mandy figured that they had just about four more hours before they got to the farmhouse. Max and Georgia had announced the plan of Georgia and her kids coming to the farmhouse with them, and Mandy felt nothing but relief upon hearing the news.

She would have another woman to talk to. She would have more people there. In numbers, there was security, at times. Max had focused so much on getting away from everyone else, Mandy had been worried that he would reject Georgia and her kids after a time. But it was clear that they weren't only not a threat, but actually an asset.

"Hey," whispered Max, sidling up next to her. They were at the front of the pack, Chad taking up the rear, his groans and explosive grunts audible all the way up there. "I don't want you to freak out, but there's someone following us.

Georgia and I saw a red shirt when we were discussing the situation earlier."

"Shit," said Mandy. "I thought we were in the clear for now."

"We're never going to be totally in the clear," said Max, keeping his voice low. "From now until we die, we're never going to be able to stop looking over our shoulders."

"Great," muttered Mandy. "Just what I need. Have you told everyone else, so that they can keep an eye out for whoever it is?"

"Yeah," said Max. "I just didn't want to tell everyone at once, in case whoever's following us is in earshot."

"Makes sense," said Mandy. "So what do we do?"

"I don't know," said Max. "For now, we're just going to have to keep our eyes peeled and not do anything stupid. Make sure to keep your gun ready at all times."

"I don't even know how to use this thing," said Mandy.

"Point and pull the trigger," said Max. "Or if worst comes to worst, just point and threaten. Pretend you know what you're doing. That might work."

"That's comforting," said Mandy sarcastically.

Max would have shrugged if he could have, but it seemed as if his pack was simply too heavy for a motion like that.

"I don't think we're going to be attacked," said Max. "We're a large group, and I think it's just one person following us."

"How do you know?"

"I guess I don't," said Max. "But I think we would have heard them if there were more people, although it's possible one person is following us and then leading a group towards us."

"What do you think they want?" said Mandy.

"Probably food," said Max. "Or our guns, our supplies. Anything, really."

"You don't think it's just some lost poor kid in the forest?"

Max shook his head. "No," he said. "Because if that was the case, if it was someone who needed help, wouldn't they just approach us?"

Mandy realized that he had a point. She felt a dark pit of terror in her stomach. She didn't like the idea of walking through the woods being followed by some unknown quantity of unknown people. It terrified her, chilled her to the bone. This was the stuff of horror movies.

"My main worry," said Max, "is that we're going to lead whoever it is right to the farmhouse."

Shit. He was right.

"That could be bad," said Mandy. "Then we're going to have to worry about being attacked there."

"Yup," said Max. "I was hoping we'd get there without anyone else knowing about the place. At least for a while, that is."

"So what are we going to do?"

"You're not going to do anything," said Max. "Except keep alert. I want the group to keep moving."

"You're planning something yourself?"

"I'm going to hang back a little," said Max. "And see if I can catch whoever it is."

"That sounds dangerous," said Mandy. "Striking out on your own like that. What if the person's armed? What if there's a group of them?"

"It's a risk I'm going to have to take," said Max. "We can't afford to hang back as a group. We need to get to the farmhouse as soon as possible. And I don't think we'll be able to catch him with more than just one person... I'll be able to move more quietly, and use the group as a distraction."

"I don't know," said Mandy. "I really don't like the idea."

"It'll be fine," said Max. "Can you let everyone else know what I'm doing? But tell them quietly, so that we're not overheard. One by one."

Mandy swallowed the lump in her throat and nodded.

"If I don't make it back," said Max, "just keep going. Get to the farmhouse, learn how to shoot properly. Georgia can teach you. And... just keep going. Don't give up. And be on the lookout in case whoever it is reaches the farmhouse. At the very least, whoever it is won't be able to follow you guys directly there. It'll buy you some more time."

Mandy was too choked up to speak. She suddenly realized that she cared for Max. She didn't want to see him go, but she knew that there was no way she could convince him otherwise. He was a headstrong individual. Once he made up his mind, he was going to follow through with his plan. She had to believe in him. She had to have confidence in him. She had to have faith that it would work out. But she couldn't rely on something as nebulous as faith. She had to make things happen. There was no fate at work out here in the woods, after the fall of civilization. Things were what you made of them, not what was handed to you.

Max stepped off the trail into the woods, pretending he was going to take a leak. He let Mandy, Georgia, James, Sadie, and Chad pass him by.

He stayed there for a moment as he watched them disappear into the woods, down the trail. They would be at the farmhouse soon enough. Hopefully he would get there too.

He was glad that Georgia was with them. She knew how to shoot properly, and it seemed like her son had some training as well. The others would be lucky to get off a single good shot if they were facing a real enemy.

There were a thousand things that could go wrong with this plan.

But Max had to do it.

He briefly considered how much his position had changed in such a short time. He'd started out only interested in helping himself. Now he was risking his own life to help the others, others he hadn't known for more than a few days, with the exception of Chad.

But Max knew that he didn't have much of a chance of

surviving on his own. Just like the others needed him, he needed them. It might be possible for him to grow his own food somehow in the future by just himself, but he knew that the possibility of actually pulling it off drastically increased with each extra person he had with him.

Max didn't think about this too long. He had other things to occupy himself with.

He still had his heavy pack on, since he couldn't have asked someone else to carry it. It would severely limit the speed at which he could travel. But at least he'd made a great effort to secure everything on the outside of the pack so that nothing rattled around. During lunch, he'd reorganized things on the inside of his pack, moving them around, putting soft things between hard metal things, to reduce the noise that he would make.

He had a compass with him, and Mandy had explained to him exactly how to get to the farmhouse through the woods. All he had to do was follow the hiking trail until he reached a certain creek. Then from there it wasn't far to the road, cutting through an old field. The farmhouse was off the road, at the end of a long private drive. In the future, Max hoped to cover the entrance to the private drive with brush. If he did that and removed any mailbox that might still be there, it would make the place almost invisible from the road.

Max had vague memories of the farmhouse as a kid, a large old building on a huge property. Not that property boundaries mattered now. But what did matter was that Max knew that the soil was good. It had been good before, and nothing had changed. It would be good in the future too.

Max held one of Georgia's rifles, and his Glock was still in its holster where it belonged.

Max had initially planned on retracing their steps, to find the person who'd been following them. But now that he was apart from the group, he realized that it would be better just to stay put. That way, he could catch whoever it was coming along the trail, without any chance of missing them.

Max set his pack down next to a tree. There were some dead leaves, and Max used them to cover the pack. He put some dead branches on top of it as well.

Then, in case someone spotted the back, he moved about twenty feet away from it, further off the trail, but still in view from it.

The hunting rifle was nothing fancy, but it worked, and it had a good, accurate scope on it.

Max, moving more freely without being burdened by the pack for the first time in a long while, lay down on his stomach. He wanted to keep himself out of view as much as possible.

He positioned the rifle comfortably in front of him, and put his eye to the scope. With its magnification, he could see much farther than he could otherwise. While that was a huge advantage, he realized that the narrow nature of the scope might cause him to miss someone coming at him from his periphery. It was the old sniper's problem, and the reason that so many snipers had lookouts there.

So Max had to play the game of putting his eye to the scope and then removing it periodically. He didn't allow himself to get stuck in just one "setting," or he knew that he could easily miss someone approaching.

Ten minutes went by, as Max lay there, diligently switching between the scope and his normal eyesight. Twenty minutes went by. Still nothing.

Then Max saw something. Off in the distance. A flash of red.

Max put his eye to the scope again. He could clearly see with the magnification a very thin man moving through the woods. He didn't seem to have a pack on him, or any gear whatsoever. He wore a red long-sleeved shirt, that must have been hot in this weather.

He had long, greasy, uncombed hair that hung down around his face.

Max paused, thinking. Who was this man? He didn't fit any profile that Max could think of.

He wasn't a soldier, and he didn't seem to have a gun. He didn't look like an ordinary citizen, with his long greasy hair. He certainly wasn't a hippie or a pothead. He was...

Then it hit Max.

The prisons.

The man must have been an escaped prisoner. That would make perfect sense. He had that gaunt look that Max had come to expect from prisoners. He'd spent some time in years past volunteering at local prisons. He'd found it valuable and interesting for a time, but gradually had given it up. Over time, Max had found that the prisoners who didn't know how to read, in large part, did not want to learn.

Max thought it through. The EMP must have damaged the prison's security system. Max imagined that any good prison would have some kind of backup generator, but that would only last for a certain amount of time. Prisons were built for power outages, but they weren't built for the end of civilization. There might have been a riot, a rebellion, or the guards might have simply abandoned the prison to tend to their own families. The doors might have simply automatically popped open, if they were electronically controlled, when the generator had stopped.

Or he might be a single lone prisoner.

There was no way to know right now.

Max looked around, his eye leaving the scope for a moment. He didn't see anyone near him.

He put his eye back to the scope, and got the crosshairs right on the gaunt man's head. Max knew he could put one right into his forehead. The man would die instantly. He wouldn't feel much pain. Just an instant of terror and confusion. And then he would be gone, dead to everything.

Max paused. Was it ethical to simply kill the man? After all, Max realized quite well that he was merely hypothesizing about his potential prisoner status.

What if the man was just like Max, Georgia, or Mandy? What if he'd been through hell the last few days, and was wandering the woods without provisions, looking for a way to survive like everyone else?

Should Max confront him, head on? That was Max's instinct, to confront the man like a man, to speak to him and to question him. But at that point, it would just be the man's word. Max would have no way of knowing if he was telling the truth or not.

He had a bad feeling about the gaunt man. A feeling deep in his gut.

Max knew the safe thing to do was to pull the trigger.

He moved his finger inside the trigger guard, feeling the trigger against the end of his index finger.

Max knew he had to shoot the man, but he didn't want to.

He hesitated just a moment too long.

He heard something off to his side, but it was already too late. Something struck him on the torso. Something sharp.

Someone was there with a knife. Max understood the situation quickly. He didn't yet feel the pain from the cut, but he knew that it was bad. It was a sort of strange background awareness he had.

Max turned, gripping the rifle with both hands, and jammed the butt as hard as he could into his attacker.

The man fell, the rifle colliding with his side. Max heard a sickening crunching sound.

Max managed to scramble up to his feet. The adrenaline was pumping through him, but he was also starting to feel the pain from the wound.

His attacker was a man with a completely shaved head. He had tattoos all over his face and his arms. He wore a wife beater t-shirt. He clearly was some kind of escaped inmate. Max's initial assessment had been correct.

Max knew that the man in the red would be approaching. Max didn't have much time. He needed to deal with this man first before the red shirted man arrived.

But Max was wounded. It was hard to move his right arm, and when he did, the pain seared through him like a red hot poker. Why couldn't the pain have taken a little longer to kick in?

The convict on the ground grunted. He opened his mouth, full of rotting teeth that had been filed down to vicious-looking points. He roared something unintelligible, some curse.

Max knew he didn't have time to waste. Holding the rifle in his left hand, he reached for his Glock and drew it.

The man sprung up from the ground in an instant, charging Max.

Max's finger squeezed the trigger, letting loose two rounds which hit the convict in the chest. He screamed and fell heavily, the holes in his chest visible through his shirt.

Before Max could do anything else, something heavy hit him in the back.

He knew who it was in an instant. It was the man in the red shirt. It felt like his fist had hit Max hard in the back.

The blow made Max reel, falling forward. He managed to catch himself from falling, stepping forward with his right leg.

The man behind him rushed Max from behind, slamming his weight into Max's back.

Max fell forward, right towards the convict he'd just shot in the chest. He held both guns as tightly as he could, knowing that he could not relinquish them.

But the convict, despite being gaunt, was surprisingly strong. He seized the rifle while Max was lying on top of the dead man. The attacker had too much leverage, since Max held the rifle with only one hand towards the muzzle. Max couldn't hold onto it for much longer. A second later, the rifle had been ripped from his hand.

Now his attacker was armed with a hunting rifle.

Max acted quickly, wasting no time in thinking.

Despite the pain, Max spun over onto his left side. He raised his right arm, pointing his Glock at his attacker, who was already raising the rifle.

Max's finger squeezed the trigger, and the Glock fired.

The round hit the attacker in the leg. Max's aim had been off from the pain, from the strange angle, from firing quickly, from being disoriented.

Max saw in slow motion as his attacker squeezed the trigger of the rifle.

Max gritted his teeth upon impact. He felt the round slam into his thigh. The pain ravaged his body, a searing hot sensation burning through his nerves.

The attacker's aim had been bad. Just like Max's first shot.

But Max wasn't going to make the same mistake twice.

He steadied his right arm as best he could, keeping the

Glock straight. He took his time. He took a deep breath and held it. He had it lined up perfectly.

Before his attacker could fire another round, Max's finger squeezed the trigger of his Glock.

The bullet hit the attacker square in the middle of his forehead. His lifeless body crumbled to the forest floor.

Max felt the intense pain. It was trying to overwhelm him, but Max wasn't going to let it. He wasn't done yet. He had to keep going.

Max lay silently on his side. It was too much effort to keep his right arm up, so he let it fall to the forest floor.

There were no more sounds. No animals. And no convicts.

Max knew it was the end of the battle.

For now.

There had just been two of them.

It was good that Max had got them before they'd gotten to the group. If the convicts had snuck up on them, it might have been disastrous.

Max struggled to stay conscious.

Finally, after what felt like an eternity, he sat up slightly to examine his leg. This seemed to take all his strength.

The wound was bleeding.

But he could still move his leg and he could still move his foot, ever so slightly.

He wasn't going to die. Not yet.

Max tore off his shirt and used it to fashion a rudimentary tourniquet, as well as a bandage. He cut the shirt into long strips and was able to use these to do what he needed to do.

The bleeding somewhat under control, Max tried to stand, but he immediately fell over. He fell with a painful thud on the ground, his head smacking into a piece of dead wood. But he shook off the pain.

OK, so he couldn't put weight on his leg.

Max looked around for something to use as a crutch. He remembered Georgia's story about fashioning a crutch from a sapling.

On all fours, moving slowly, Max moved to a small sapling. He took his pocket knife from his pocket and sawed at the sapling's base. It seemed to take forever, but in the end, he had a serviceable crutch.

Max wrapped some fabric around the end of it, to make it less painful as it stuck into his armpit.

It wasn't perfect, but Max wasn't going to bleed out immediately, and he could move.

He recovered the rifle, slung it over his shoulder, made sure his Glock was in its holster, and went to recover his pack.

He knew intuitively that he couldn't carry the pack all the way back, at least not the way it was currently loaded down.

Max opened the pack and started discarding things that wouldn't be essential. That was the idea, at least. But unfortunately so much of what he had was essential. But he simply wasn't going to be able to carry it all.

He knew he needed to get to the farmhouse. It might take him a very long time, given how difficult it was for him to walk. He kept extra ammo for the Glock and the rifle. He kept food and water, which he would need for the journey. He kept the water filters that they would need in the future. He kept his emergency medical kit, which he didn't bother trying to use now, since he knew that he didn't know what he was doing with it, and he didn't know what else he could do now for a gunshot wound.

It was only in thinking of the medical kit that Max remembered being cut. He paused to examine the wound. It wasn't as bad as he'd initially thought. It was a long cut, but it wasn't deep, and the bleeding had mostly stopped.

Max took the provisions that he wasn't bringing along, which was the majority of what had been in the pack, and carefully buried it under the same leaves he'd used to cover the pack. He took his pocket knife out and carved a single line in one of the trees, to serve as a marker for some future date. In the future, he could come back and recover the provisions. There might come a time when they meant the difference between life and death.

Shouldering his lightened pack, gritting his teeth against the pain, Max set off, limping with his crutch. His eyes studied the forest around him, and he was alert. He listened to the sounds. He wasn't going to be ambushed, no matter what condition he was in.

"I think that's it," said Mandy, pointing ahead.

The five of them had emerged from the woods and were standing in an overgrown field. It had been a good solid two hours of hiking from where they'd left Max.

They gazed across the field at the house.

It was a farm house all right, but it looked like it hadn't been used in years. All of the windows were boarded up with wood.

"I can't believe we got here," said Chad, who had arrived, panting a little, after the others. He immediately threw his pack down and flopped onto the ground.

The others were tired and hungry.

Mandy felt mixed emotions on getting "home."

In one way, the journey was over. She hoped it had been the most difficult part, but she knew that it wasn't. She knew that a thousand challenges would crop up in the future.

And the house… it wasn't as if she was expecting a castle. But she had been expecting a house that looked a little more… serviceable.

"It's not too bad," said Georgia, standing next to Mandy.

"Are we going to really live *there*?" said Sadie.

"Shut up, Sadie," said James. "At least we're going to have a place to live. And we can grow food here. You do like food, don't you?"

"*How* are we going to grow food?" said Sadie, her voice full of snark.

Mandy knew that she had a point. Getting seeds or animals was going to be a monumental task. She didn't even know where they were going to start.

"I hope Max is OK," said Chad from the ground.

Mandy hoped so too. Without Max there, she felt lost. She'd led the group quite capably to the farmhouse, but she now realized that they'd all been looking to Max for direction, for what to do next. Max always seemed to have a plan, no matter how bad things were.

"Well," said Mandy. "Let's go check it out."

Everyone kept their rifles out in front of them. They knew at this point not to expect the best.

Chad groaned as he got up.

The house actually looked a little better the closer they got to it. The old white paint was peeling, but the house looked solid.

They set their packs down outside, and they decided that Mandy and Georgia would enter first.

"Ladies," said Chad. "Excuse me, but if anyone should go in first, it should be me."

They were surprised. It turned out that Chad really had turned over a new leaf. He was willing to potentially sacrifice himself for the good of the others.

Chad held his rifle in front of him, ready to fire it at close range without the scope if necessary. His pack was laying outside with the rest of them.

The door wasn't boarded up, and Mandy opened it for him. It hadn't even been locked.

Chad took a step inside, before calling out, "I can't see anything in here."

"I'll come in," said Mandy, taking a flashlight Max had loaned her.

She walked behind Chad, holding the flashlight so they could see clearly. Some daylight came in little streams through the boarded up windows. But whoever had boarded the windows had done a very thorough job, and it wasn't enough light to see by.

"This actually is pretty nice," said Mandy.

To her surprise, the house was still full of things you would expect in an older house. There were plates in the kitchen, spoons in the drawers. There were bookshelves with books in the living room, and there were beds in all the upstairs rooms.

There was even canned food in the basement. There were cans of peaches, tomatoes, and even pickles.

"I'm getting hungry just looking at all this," said Chad.

Mandy laughed.

The danger of a possible intruder in the house seemed to have passed. They spent some time exploring the house before heading back into the sunshine to join the others.

"It's better than we expected," said Mandy. "There's even food in there."

"Nice," said James.

"I just hope Max makes it back soon," said Georgia, eyeing the sky.

Mandy knew what she was thinking: the sun was going to set soon, and it would be more dangerous out there at night. Not to mention more difficult to find the way.

But Max had a flashlight. And he was smart. He would make it back, Mandy was sure of it.

They set about bringing their packs and their gear into the living room of the house. It was strange to see the survival gear and the hiking backpacks sitting on the nice carpet of the living room, next to an old fashioned ornate sofa, with hardbound books on the shelves.

"I don't understand why this stuff is still here," said Sadie, looking at the books.

"Come on, Sadie," said Georgia. "There's still work to be done. You can look at the books later. Give me a hand with the cooking."

With her flashlight, Mandy found some candles in the kitchen drawer, along with some matches.

She was about to bring them back to Georgia so she could get started with the cooking, and to put them around the house where they might need them.

Only at the last moment did she realize that she was in what was actually a kitchen. She tried the stove.

To her absolute surprise, when she turned the knob, gas came out of the burner. She lit it with her match and sure enough, it continued to burn.

"Georgia!" she called out. "Come look at this!"

Georgia and Sadie came into the room.

"Wow," said Georgia. "I can barely believe it."

"Well I guess we shouldn't get used to it," said Mandy. "I suppose it's a tank that'll run out eventually."

"Let's just enjoy it while we can," said Georgia.

Mandy turned off the gas to conserve it, while Georgia and Sadie rooted around in the cupboard to see what kinds of pots and pans they had.

Unfortunately, no water came out of the tap.

"Maybe it's just shut off," said Mandy.

"Maybe," said Georgia.

"Do you think the city water will still be running?"

"This place is probably on a well," said Georgia.

"Yeah," said Mandy, agreeing, but she realized her mind really wasn't on the cooking. Her mind was on Max. Part of her wanted to go look for him, but Max had warned her specifically against that. He'd said it would be too dangerous, and that they needed to stay together as a group. The worst thing that could happen, Max had said, was that the group further fragmented.

Mandy left Georgia, Sadie, and a rather reluctant James, to get down to cooking. They had to improvise quite a bit, because the remaining perishable foods at this point were varied. There was a bit of chicken left, some bacon, a single egg, half a stick of butter. It was a hodgepodge, but it would work. They would be fed. For now.

"No sign of Max?" said Mandy, sitting down on the front porch steps next to Chad, who'd been guarding the house from the outside.

The sun had set, and darkness was settling over the land.

"Nope," said Chad, looking across the field into the distance. "Not that I'd be able to see him right now anyway."

"You think he'll make it?" said Mandy.

Chad nodded. "I'm sure of it," he said. "Ever since he was a little kid, he's been a tough old bastard. He can deal with anything."

"So what's the story between you two?" said Mandy. "Some kind of childhood rivalry or something?"

"It's not complicated," said Chad. "We were good friends, and then I got into drugs. That's pretty much it."

Mandy didn't say anything. She didn't know what to say, and she was learning that sometimes no words were needed.

After half an hour, Georgia called out that the food was ready.

Mandy joined them inside, where they ate in the dining room at the table. Chad remained outside, insisting that he stand guard. Georgia sent James to bring some food to him.

"It's strange to be sitting around a table like civilized people again," said Mandy.

"I like it," said Sadie.

"What about you, James?" said Mandy.

James had been conspicuously silent all day, all through the walk.

"It's nice," said James. "I'm just worried about what we're going to eat in the future."

"We'll figure it out," said Georgia. "Remember, your mother's quite the hunter."

"But we only have so many bullets," said James.

"We'll figure something out," said Georgia. "There's more than one way to skin a cat."

When the meal was finished, Mandy went back outside to join Chad on the porch.

"Still no sign of him?"

"Nope," was all Chad said.

She could hear it in his voice. Chad was worried about his friend. Just like she was.

Mandy realized that she'd assumed Max would be there with them, his comforting, strong presence, his leadership. But maybe he wouldn't make it...

She realized that she'd assumed that she and Max would become a couple. It had happened quickly, this change in mindset, and it had become something of a background thought that she merely assumed...

Now, though, she wasn't so sure. He might not make it back.

After a couple hours of waiting on the porch, Chad told her that she'd better get inside and get some rest. He assured her that he was fine to stay up. He still couldn't sleep right because of not having his pills. The stuff was out of his system, but it would be a long time before his body was back to normal.

But Mandy stayed on the porch with him, refusing to budge, even when Georgia came out and asked her to come inside.

"I'm just going to wait out here a little longer," said Mandy.

Georgia nodded, and went back inside with her kids.

Chad and Mandy didn't speak through the night.

Mandy's mind was filled with a thousand thoughts. She thought about the future, how they would survive out here, how they would grow their food, how they would defend themselves against the hordes of people that Max had assured her would come from the city.

But most of all she thought of Max.

The hours of the night passed. Long, dark hours. The animals were awake, making noises. Mandy heard the hoot of an owl, and movement off in the distance. Towards dawn, they heard the birds waking up, singing their songs.

The sky was cloudless, and the moon faintly illuminated the fields in front of them, all the way to the edge of the forest. Their eyes slowly adjusted to the darkness, giving them good night vision.

The sounds were not what Mandy was used to. Back in her suburban life, the only sounds she'd heard at night were cars speeding by on the highway. And the occasional bird in the morning, of course. But the sounds in the suburbs were nothing like the sounds out here. If this had been a vacation, Mandy would have felt relaxed. And that was the strange thing—this was just the sort of place one might come for a relaxing vacation, to get away from it all.

The sun was rising, and Mandy was still awake.

"You still awake?" said Chad.

Mandy just grunted her acknowledgement.

"He'll be here soon," said Chad, trying to comfort her. He seemed to understand her feelings for Max.

But Mandy didn't see how he could possibly come back. It should have only taken him a few hours at the most. But it had been all night.

"Hey," said Chad, poking her. "Look!"

Mandy lifted her tired head and looked to where Chad was no pointing.

At the edge of the overgrown field, there was Max.

It was definitely him. Mandy felt she would recognize him from any distance.

He was emerging from the forest.

Her heart leapt as she saw him.

But something was wrong. He wasn't walking right.

"He's limping!" said Mandy.

She got up off the steps quickly and ran towards Max.

Chad followed, his heavy footsteps falling at a distance.

"Max!" cried out Mandy.

33

MAX

Max woke up in a bed, the morning light streaming in through the window. He looked at the window, and saw that the glass was cracked, but not totally broken. Below the window sill lay some wooden boards that he guessed had been used to board up the window. Someone had removed them.

Max felt better than he had all week. His body was recuperating, as he'd hoped.

He moved his leg under the sheets, straightening it. It felt stiff, but it was good he could move it. Hopefully soon he would be able to walk easily. For now, he was confined to the bed. He hated being in this position. He didn't like feeling like he was an imposition to everyone else, even though they all assured him that that wasn't the case.

When Max had first arrived at the farm house, he hadn't thought that he was going to make it. His vision had been blurry and he could barely see the house, let alone a few feet in front of him. His vision had swum and he'd been so filled with pain that he was sure he couldn't take another step.

It had taken him all night to make the short hike. He'd needed frequent breaks, sitting down on the trail, lying down, whatever it took to gain just a little bit more energy, to have a slight break from the constant pain in his leg. As he'd continued walking, the wound had bled. The more he had walked, the more it had bled, but there was nothing he could do about it except tighten the tourniquet and grit his teeth against the horrible searing pain that rocked through him, burning his body like a high-powered laser.

If someone had come along, another convict, Max would have been done for. But he had been lucky. He hadn't met anyone on the trail.

He remembered Mandy and Chad running towards him. He remembered hands carrying him into the farm house. He remembered someone pouring alcohol down his throat, some type of harsh vodka that burned his mouth, but helped a little with the pain. They'd laid him out on the dining room table and Max vaguely remembered Georgia using a kitchen knife to cut away his clothes entirely, as Mandy bent over him and checked the wounds. He remembered how frantic everyone had acted, how worried they'd been. The last thing he remembered was Mandy leaning over him with a pair of medical forceps.

Mandy had filled him in on the details after he'd woken up a day later. She'd grabbed a medical field guide that Georgia had with her. She'd learned on the spot how to remove a bullet from a body, and apparently she'd done a good enough job because Max was still alive, and he was sure that his leg was healing nicely.

"How you feeling?" said Mandy, poking her head into the room.

"Good," said Max, grinning at her. "Thanks to you."

She blushed. "You keep going on about the impromptu

surgery," she said. "But it's nothing you wouldn't have done for me."

"I just don't think I would have been able to pull it off successfully," said Max.

Mandy laughed. "Who knows," she said. "Hopefully we won't have to do any more surgeries on the dining room table."

"How's the day looking?" said Max.

"Good," said Mandy. "Chad's been up since before dawn organizing the food."

"How's it looking?"

Mandy seemed to force a grin. "We've got about a month left," she said. "And now that the well is bringing water through the pipes, we've got enough water for..."

"For a while, hopefully," said Max.

"Yeah," said Mandy. "I don't know anything about wells, and was hoping you did."

"Sorry," said Max, shrugging. "I don't. I guess to be safe, we should find a nearby stream or something."

"We need to check the water filters," said Mandy. But she looked at Max, and seemed to see that he was just as worried as she was about all these things. "But don't worry about that now, Max. You just need to get your strength back. We're getting on fine without you."

Max knew that Mandy knew he wanted to be up and active, helping out. That was just his nature.

But Max also knew that he wouldn't be much good to anyone if he didn't let his leg properly heal.

"No sign of any more convicts?" said Max.

"No," said Mandy, shaking her head.

"It's only a matter of time," said Max.

"We'll be prepared," said Mandy, a look of determination on her face. "Chad, James, and Sadie have been working on digging a trench."

"Good," said Max.

"Let's see how that leg's doing," said Mandy, approaching the bed.

She pulled the sheet back and studied Max's leg.

"Looking good," she said. "No black spots or anything."

"Dr. Mandy approves?" said Max.

She nodded and smiled at him.

She leaned down, and Max reached up and pulled her closer to him. His mouth met hers, and they shared a deep, passionate kiss.

"Well," said Mandy, blushing as she pulled away, straightening up. "I'd better get back to see how Georgia's doing in the kitchen. I'll bring your breakfast soon."

Max just smiled at her as she left the room. He reached for a book that had been lying on the bedside table. He'd been reading it all yesterday. It was a field guide to edible plants native to their area of Pennsylvania.

Max's eyes sank into the words as he absorbed them. He knew that this book might hold the key to surviving the coming winter.

There were many obstacles that they faced—hunger, escaped convicts, the hordes leaving the cities.

Max had always possessed that grim determination that had served him well so far. But for the first time since the EMP, Max actually felt optimistic about their chances.

THE END

ABOUT RYAN WESTFIELD

Ryan Westfield is an author of post-apocalyptic survival thrillers. He's always had an interest in "being prepared," and spends time wondering what that really means. When he's not writing and reading, he enjoys being outdoors.

Contact Ryan at ryanwestfieldauthor@gmail.com

MAILING LIST

Sign up for my mailing list to receive information on new releases: http://eepurl.com/c23NmT

Made in the USA
Lexington, KY
17 June 2018